WATERLOO SUNSET

Ray Davies was born in north London. Together with his younger brother, Dave, he launched the Kinks in February 1964. Their first number one hit single, 'You Really Got Me', was followed by thirty albums and a series of hit singles, including 'Waterloo Sunset' and 'Lola'. Ray Davies has also worked in television, film and the theatre and has written songs for other well-known pop musicians. He lives in London. His first book, *X-Ray*, his autobiography, is also published by Penguin.

RAY DAVIES
WATERLOO SUNSET

PENGUIN BOOKS

PENGUIN BOOKS

Published by the Penguin Group
Penguin Books Ltd, 27 Wrights Lane, London w8 5tz, England
Penguin Putnam Inc., 375 Hudson Street, New York, New York 10014, USA
Penguin Books Australia Ltd, Ringwood, Victoria, Australia
Penguin Books Canada Ltd, 10 Alcorn Avenue, Toronto, Ontario, Canada m4v 3b2
Penguin Books (NZ) Ltd, 182–190 Wairau Road, Auckland 10, New Zealand

Penguin Books Ltd, Registered Offices: Harmondsworth, Middlesex, England

First published by Viking 1997
Published with a Preface in Penguin 1998
10 9 8 7 6 5 4 3 2 1

Permission to reproduce the following lyrics is gratefully acknowledged: 'Scattered', published by
Carlin Music, copyright © Ray Davies, 1992. 'Rock and Roll Fantasy', published by Carlin Music,
copyright © Ray Davies, 1977. 'Mr Pleasant', published by Carlin Music, copyright © Ray Davies,
1967. 'Celluloid Heroes', published by Carlin Music, copyright © Ray Davies, 1976. 'Voices in the
Dark', published by Carlin Music, copyright © Ray Davies, 1985. 'Holiday Romance', published by
Carlin Music, copyright © Ray Davies, 1975. 'Art Lover', published by Carlin Music, copyright ©
Ray Davies, 1981. 'Still Searching', published by Carlin Music, copyright © Ray Davies, 1990. 'Return
To Waterloo', published by Carlin Music, copyright © Ray Davies, 1993. 'Going Solo', published
by Carlin Music, copyright © Ray Davies, 1985. 'Afternoon Tea', published by Carlin Music,
copyright © Ray Davies, 1967. 'The Million-Pound Semi-Detached', published by Carlin Music,
copyright © Ray Davies, 1990. 'My Diary', copyright © Ray Davies, 1994. 'Driving', published by
Carlin Music, copyright © Ray Davies, 1969.

The moral right of the author has been asserted

Set in Monotype Bembo
Printed in England by Clays Ltd, St Ives plc

Contents

Foreword

It's a great feeling whenever a record company asks me to go into the studio to record a new album. It's flattering to think that people still want my music, gratifying to know that there is still an audience out there. The only problem is that before you make a record, you've got to have the songs – the material, ideas, the hooks and riffs, the lyrics and music. This should be easy. After all, writing songs is fun – isn't it? Unfortunately, sometimes the journey to that final piece of 'fun' is littered with wrecked relationships, unsavoury deeds and unscrupulous people. On these occasions the need to meet deadlines, the desire to succeed, to write great 'stuff' that will live up to everyone's expectations invariably outweighs the joy in the end result. The final cut is never sufficient reward. That's why I created the character of Lester Mulligan. In many ways he embodies all the fears and anxieties I live through when I am trying to write a new album. I created him because people would not believe my reality. They would rather attach these bizarre events to a fictitious person – particularly when that person seems rather unbalanced.

The question I get asked more than any other is what comes first, the words or the music. Each time, it makes me stop and think. I wish I had an explanation, some words of wisdom, but I don't. For my own part, I usually write alone. I don't have a co-writer tinkling away on a piano while I pace up and down, searching for words. Nor do I sit at the piano with a poem already prepared. There are no rules to the way I work. No plan. But if I were pushed, I'd have to say that the best ideas come when the words and music happen at the same time. I sometimes carry an idea around in my head for months, maybe years, until I find a home for it or a character to attach it to, as if I'm the custodian of a lost spirit looking for a song to inhabit. The images turn to plots, to plays that will never be performed, because once they have been used to produce a song, they will be abandoned. This process has served to move me from one record to another, but just the same I can't help feeling that there might be a lot of unhappy and unfulfilled characters out there in the creative void. That's why it's a relief when I eventually find a home for these lost souls. It's a catastrophe when, like in the song 'Return to Waterloo', they are miscast, but I am usually aware enough to correct the error before these 'creatures' are unleashed. When the components jell, it's like an explosion. I'm always amazed when the bits come together. It's an unconscious thing, I instinctively know that the items add up. Then I have it — a total idea. There is no time-frame. One year I had a busy tour schedule and there was only one clear day that could be allocated to writing songs. The rest of the time I wrote in 'transit' or woke in a hotel room with an idea for a song in my head. The ideas take the form of character studies, stories, films, or even simple images. With an image, I see what's happening. The faces are there, and the players act out one of my fantasies, which eventually ends up as a song. It is then that I make a demo, a rough, inexpensive and usually not very high quality recording of a song to use as a guide for other musicians or record companies. Demos are sketches, a first draft. The vocals are foggy and the music is low-fi, with cotton-wool guitars. Because they are imperfect, they have a charm; for me, demos are the most sensitive, appealing version of the song. They do not aim for technical perfection; they are raw, naked and innocent. Then the demo is rearranged to suit the musicians. They change the parts, 'improve' it and make it theirs. The mechanical world gets hold of the song, introducing dynamics and the technology which is supposed to make it fit for human consumption. The 'better' it begins to sound, the less the song is mine. I've lost it.

This book of stories is more about the thought process behind rather than the actual construction of the songs. It is not meant to be autobiographical – at least, I didn't intend it to be so when I started writing it – but the character often dictates the style, taking me into unchartered territory. This, as you might discover when you read these stories, can be an unnerving experience. At times, I get so involved in my songs that I feel there is some strange voodoo thing happening. Many of the dark characters in them, and in these stories, have elements of me in them. That's a worry. Others are composites of people I have known. Lester Mulligan links many of the stories, and there are parallels between us too. I have experienced many of his insecurities, have gone through the humiliation of people saying to me that my new songs are not as good as the ones I used to write for my band. (As grateful as I am for those old hits, as proud as I am of them and the happy memories they bring to me and to other people, I often wish I could be accepted more for the songs I write now.) My characters are like companions who help me deal with the real world. They help me confront issues that I find too hard to face.

As for the songs on which the stories are based, the demos have always been better than the finished records. Lester Mulligan will always be dissatisfied until he can find a way of showing his ideas in their totality; until then, his life will be like a record, not as good as the demo. As for myself, I don't have so much of a problem with accepting my creative fate. When the Kinks recorded 'Waterloo Sunset' I hadn't actually made a demo before we went into the studio. The finished record *was* the demo. I couldn't admit it then because the mechanical world might have asked me to make a definitive version. So, in many ways, I had it all my own way, and people loved it. So, whatever happens, I will always have the satisfaction of knowing that in that instance things worked out. At least that particular story had a happy ending.

–Ray Davies, 1998

The Shirt

It could have been 1968. The view from the fifth-floor balcony of the Hyatt Hotel on Sunset hadn't changed. Les had first stayed there at a time when Frank Zappa and the Mothers held court at the International House of Pancakes and Ben Frank's coffee shop and Charlie Manson was still contemplating how to become a celebrity. It could have been 1968. Wild Man Fisher would still be walking up and down the Strip singing his new album a cappella to anyone who would listen or maybe give him a deal. The GTOs would be hanging out with various bands while they waited for their singing careers to take off. Zeppelin would have been playing the Forum. Jethro Tull would already have checked out and flown up to Frisco. And Les would have been picked up at the airport and delivered to the hotel in a limo. He would have been a big star then, and Miss Pamela of Girls Together Outrageous would have been hot in pursuit.

Downtown LA was covered in a slight haze, the fog not as thick as it had been in the past. The unreal, optimistic sun was still bright enough to put a pink filter over an overcast day and giant billboards advertised cabaret acts in Las Vegas alongside the latest movie releases. Over the years, the restaurant on the sidewalk opposite had been through the changes. Originally a breakfast joint, then a mid-priced diner, a cocktail bar. In the early eighties it had cut its losses and settled for being a fast-food eatery. It had gone full cycle, and Les felt his career had gone the same way. He catered for people's tastes, and in his world, the world of popular music, tastes

3

changed fast. As a songwriter Les had learned to become a pretty versatile chef.

He'd grown up in a large family of part-Irish, part-Welsh descent, with even a touch of French on his grandfather's side. It had been mainly English, though, English working class. He had been christened Leslie Mulligan, but when he heard the blues record 'Naggin' Woman' by Lazy Lester, he'd changed his name by deed poll. When he'd left his group to go solo he'd used the stage name 'Mulligan'. More rock and roll than 'Les Mulligan', but it never quite cut it beside 'Mick Jagger' or 'Bob Dylan'. 'Mulligan' had some charisma, but early on he found himself confused with the jazz saxophonist, or assumed to be an Irish folk singer specializing in anti-British dirges. He'd been booked in to some dodgy Irish pub in north-west London, and when he started singing his songs about the English countryside, silence had fallen. Someone put a country and western song on the jukebox and this, combined with the clatter of the fruit machines, had drowned him out. That gig had been the absolute low of Les's career. He went back to billing himself 'the former lead singer of' so he could sing his old hits and get some decent bookings. He was so used to touring with the same band that the sudden shock of being out there on his own plunged him into crisis. It was almost as if he had to change his identity in order to perform as himself. That's when he'd become emotionally unhinged. That's when he started to bow out of the conventional music scene and depart on his own eccentric journey, to commercial oblivion. It wasn't until one of his old hits was covered by a punk band in the late eighties that people remembered him. That's when the world started to ask if Les Mulligan was still alive. When Richard Tennant decided to track him down.

A couple of miles away at a plush Beverly Hills hotel, Richard Tennant was complaining about the size of his room. The potted plants had not been watered and the leaves were dry and turning brown at the ends. The air-conditioning system made a rattling noise, and the pink and blue décor of his room made it look like a 'tart's boudoir'. Richard complained louder. The assistant manager arrived to defuse the situation and ensure that the aptly named guest was relocated satisfactorily. Richard lit another cigarette and complained that there were no ashtrays in the room. When the grovelling assistant manager explained that the suite was non-smoking, Richard glared, and took another large gasp of Marlboro into his lungs.

Despite his complaints, Richard knew the hotel deal was hard to beat. Two bedrooms with en suite bathrooms, private sauna and jacuzzi, dining area with antique furniture, all for the price of a single room. Richard Tennant was a rich businessman, but the cheapness of the deal still gratified him. He'd flown first class; it was what he deserved, his right. Part payment for having to do a job he hated, mixing in circles where the people bored and repelled him. He'd thought his days of hustling were over and he could run his little financial empire via a mobile phone and fax machine from a yacht moored off Bermuda. But he hadn't predicted the Wall Street Crash of 87, or the financial undoings of Lloyds, where he had been one of those mysteriously unlucky 'names'. And he'd fallen foul of the property boom. It was time to make another fortune, and quickly. There were still artists out there who needed to cut deals – rich pickings for shrewd businessmen like Richard. He poured the tea, adding just enough milk to turn it murky brown, took out his toilet bag and swigged down a couple of anti-depressants. His fifth cigarette, and he would be ready for the day.

Les had slept badly. He had amassed enough frequent-flyer points to fly to LA for free, but the flight had arrived late and by the time he'd got into Hollywood most of the restaurants had closed. He'd checked into his room and taken a cab down La Cienaga and along the length of Melrose Avenue, but he'd forgotten what an early town LA was. Back at the hotel he'd taken a sleeping pill, but it hadn't worked. He'd tried to masturbate, failed, taken another sleeper. This time he went off, but woke in the night in a paranoid sweat. He must have stayed in the same mini suite at least ten times before, and in his sweat, the years squeezed his body like a concertina. Did he have a gig? Was it 1972? 1982? By the time he finished searching in the darkness for the television remote, he realized he hadn't done a gig in LA for five years. The telephone woke him at 8 a.m. He'd forgotten what an early town LA was.

Richard Tennant's deep voice sounded more upper class and out of place than usual.

'I thought I'd track you down there. I'll be over to pick you up for dinner, say, at 7.30 this evening.'

Les was happy to have some time to sleep off his jet lag and psych himself up. He would need all day to get his mind into some sort of order, to be ready to see Richard and listen to his proposal. He hadn't wanted the meeting, but he'd had no choice. The bank was asking questions about his overdraft, and the alimony on his last marriage was well overdue. Richard had jumped the gun and organized some meetings for the following week too. Inconvenient for Les, but maybe something would come of them.

The lobby was full of posers schmoozing before a concert at the Forum. Les hid in the bar. Richard's Mercedes pulled up dead on time, and Les felt somehow relieved to see him. There was some banter about how dull LA seemed compared to New York, where Les had an apartment. Apart from that they didn't speak. They had nothing in common. They each wore classically cut shirts from a gentlemen's outfitter in Burlington Arcade, near Savile Row, but Richard's was tailor-made and Les's off the peg. The labels matched.

Both men were middle aged and were considered veterans in the music industry. Richard was a manager-cum-dealmaker with the knack of maximizing record companies' advances and getting a good deal for the artists he represented as well as securing himself a healthy slice by way of commission. For Richard, the music was secondary. The deal was all. Art was a means to an end and every creative thought had its price. He fixed the tariff. Of course he couldn't tell his clients that – and definitely not this client. He was dealing with a temperamental artist, known to be sensitive and sometimes volatile. Mulligan, or Les, as he insisted on being called privately, was known to be particularly sensitive about financial and contractual issues. He had fallen out with industry people before, but now, in leaner times, he had learned to tolerate entrepreneurs like Richard.

Richard had been off the scene for nearly a decade but had recently bounced back with a series of dazzling deals, securing financial remuneration far in excess of the value of the artists he represented. He was, all the breeding and good manners of an Englishman aside, a good old-fashioned hustler. Breeding helped, though. Richard felt that his upper-class manner alone was worth the commission. He looked upon Les as an investment, and had compiled a complete dossier on him, his potential new venture. Lester Mulligan. Huge in the sixties, wayward in the mid seventies, over to the States for a creative renaissance in the early eighties. Then, some time in 1984, everything had suddenly come to a halt. There was a rumour that he had died, and then – that punk single. Richard knew Les would be shopping for a new contract. Unlike many of the artists he represented, he actually believed Les to be a formidable talent and a platform on which to build up younger artists. They'd be impressed that Richard was Les Mulligan's manager. It would be arduous tracking him down, in the bars and brasseries of various cities, but the fat slice of a record deal at the end of the line would make it worth while. Richard finally traced him to his seedy New York apartment. Everyone in the business knew that Les had been through some kind of identity crisis in the mid eighties, so Richard was cautious in his initial approach. He had courted Les for some time, through numerous expensive restaurants, a weekend at Richard's house in Sussex, a rescue from a scuffle with a pretty waitress after too much Dom Perignon in a New York piano bar. He'd come to know the songwriter. Too much time living in America, too many years in a slump, too much time at the doors of casualty. He'd heard Les rant on about the importance of retaining his artistic credibility, his lost opportunities, betrayals by trusted employees, his ravaged personal life. Richard would raise an eyebrow and order another bottle of wine. He'd heard the same tales of woe from many a sixties has-been.

Richard was at the wheel, the songwriter captive in his Mercedes, heading across the Hollywood hills to a sleek restaurant adorned with film- and music-biz insiders. He came straight to the point. He needed some kind of sneak preview, some idea of 'the product' before he could go for a big advance. There was an air of pragmatic detachment in the way he spoke, a clinical assessment of market value delivered with the cold efficiency of a surgeon's scalpel. Two or three companies would pay, but, in Richard's opinion, there was only one really serious player. The smaller companies were nothing more than boutiques and would either go under or get eaten up by the bigger distributors. Richard began his carefully rehearsed speech.

'You've been signed to most of the majors during your career, and I know that United Records would see you, with your track record and back catalogue, as a valuable acquisition. Your recent albums haven't sold too well, and you do have this reputation of being difficult. But, if the proposal is put together properly. I see no reason why we can't ask for, say, ten million up front with provision for a bonus structure when the new product sells. Which brings me to the main point, Les. Are you going to let me represent you?'

Les looked ahead as the car turned a corner to reveal a breathtaking view of Los Angeles. While Richard seemed to know everything about his new client, Les had been able to find out very little about

Richard. People in the business knew the name but little else. A couple blurted out that anyone who got involved with Richard Tennant was bound to end up in court, drug and alcohol rehab, or a mental hospital. But that could just be the business. Les did talk to one helpful ex-music-publisher who had once administered a company for Richard. This was in the late sixties, when Richard was a tax exile. There was some litigation over sub-publishing rights, and Tennant had returned them to the writer he was in dispute with. A very rare occurrence in the music-publishing world. When Les brought the story up, he was amazed that Richard made light of it. He seemed almost embarrassed by his benevolent gesture, as if it was bad form for a businessman to show his good side. That side had impressed Les, even though the same publisher had warned Les about Tennant's dubious partners in Miami. Les couldn't imagine anyone with Tennant's upbringing having any connections with organized crime, and couldn't ask Richard directly. Anyway, he had sold himself on the idea that Richard Tennant could deliver the goods, and the less negative information Les knew about him, the better. The industry, for the most part, never had a good word to say for anybody.

'To tell you the truth, Richard, I've asked around, and I can't find two people to say a good word for you.'

Richard barely flinched and carefully manoeuvred his Mercedes around a solitary jogger.

'Don't get me wrong. I like you. You know I need to make a deal to kickstart my career, but at this stage I need reassurance that the deal will be managed and not just brokered. If it's only a deal-making situation, I may as well have an attorney do it for me.'

Richard remained calm. He smiled and took out another cigarette. 'That's if they can get a foot in the door at United Records.'

Les was surprised by Richard's confidence. United was the biggest company on the planet.

'You mean you know the people at United?'

'I had drinks with Annette Fabrizzi in their business department. She thought the German owners would go for the deal. Also Morton Sosa, who runs the US operation, likes the idea, and since he failed to lure the Rolling Stones to the label, he needs to sign an act with a back catalogue to show his Aryan masters that no one is indispensable. It'll be a major coup for him.'

It was a long time since Les had been flattered in this way. It was reassuring to hear that a major company was this interested. Even so, he stuck to his guns.

'That's great to hear, Richard. But we do have this problem with your credibility. You can't blame me for wanting some sort of . . .'

Richard cut him off.

'Good conduct report. You'll never get that.'

'Then give me a reason why I should let you do the deal for me.'

Richard smiled. He had done his research.

'You need the money desperately. If you were a company you would have been taken over or made bankrupt by now. You have cash-flow problems, and I recognize and appreciate your need for cash. Plus the fact that you've been pissed on by most people in the music industry and haven't had all the breaks you should have had. Now I've come along to remedy the situation.'

Richard parked the Mercedes, and they walked into the restaurant, which was nestled among pine trees in countrified seclusion. The waiters all spoke Italian, but looked like they had been recruited from a Scandinavian stud farm, given dark suntans, and had pistols ready to dispose of any unwanted guests. Richard had enjoyed his speech and knocked back a gin and tonic in one go. Les just sat and played with his glass. Richard had obviously struck a nerve. As dinner progressed, Les tried to gain some ground. The wine was flowing and the conversation started to pick up. Les knew that he was in a weak position but still wanted Richard to feel that it was him who was being scrutinized.

'Where did you go to school, Richard?'

'Eton.'

'I went to a state secondary in North London. We've got different upbringings, different styles.'

Richard sensed a wind-up, but needed some entertainment after two bottles of Chianti.

'But you went to college afterwards. Don't try that working-man crap with me. My word, college. I say, you're almost middle class.'

Les felt like snapping back but refused to be rattled.

'I went to college because I was talented. It was nothing to do with privilege. In any event, that's beside the point. What soccer team do you support?' Don't tell me. You don't even like soccer. We have nothing in common.'

'Where do you buy your shirts, Les?'

'Hilditch and Key.'

'That's something we have in common.'

Richard *had* done his research. He took the opportunity to score another point off the songwriter.

'You mean you don't shop at Marks and Spencer's after all? Better not let your fans find out. Could ruin the image.'

Les managed a wry smile and started on the third bottle of wine. The tension eased as they sparred over various proposals for the deal. Les wanted a 'British' deal. America had a stranglehold on the business and had squeezed out the innocence. It had corrupted the industry by throwing out huge advances in the eighties. Richard started talking about the sort of numbers normally found in the telephone directory. You could only get those sorts of deal from an American company, and then only if they had some idea of 'the product'.

'They'll need a demo.'

Les spilled some clam sauce down his shirt. Richard sounded as if he had doubts. Les compounded them by looking a little embarrassed and admitting that he hadn't written anything for some time.

He felt comfortable enough with Richard now to tell him that the mere thought of writing another song filled him with fear. How making his last album had nearly given him a nervous breakdown. Sometimes even the thought of going into the studio made him want to see a shrink. A cold stare hovered between disbelief and disgust on Richard's face. He eased out a glimmer of a smile, reassuring Les that he'd soon get into the creative swing of things once the deal was done. Les was less convinced. He explained that he had always vetted his demo tapes before playing them to anyone. He'd had difficult experiences in the past; the songs took on lives of their own and overpowered him. Some of them took on a semi-religious aura, others seemed touched by an evil spirit. Once he'd kept such a song locked in his basement until he felt that the spirit had departed. Another time, he'd sought witches' help to drive out the demons. At other times, though, a song had helped him through a difficult patch. Through the death of a friend or the break-up of a relationship. Songs about broken love and hard times getting better. Simple, uncluttered songs about relationships that people could associate with. Richard was convinced now that Les had been a casualty, but didn't let on. Les was talking about a song that had sown a bad seed in him. When Richard asked which song it had been, Les took another bite of his pasta. At last he was ahead of the game. He had something Richard wanted. In a burst of paranoia Les began to think that Richard would use his secrets to control him, as a hold over him. He wouldn't give away the song, but he wanted to talk about what had happened.

'Have you ever been confronted by a replica of yourself? Something that shattered your belief in yourself?'

Richard was trying to understand what Les was talking about.

'You mean a clone or a doppelgänger?'

Les gulped down what remained of his armagnac, and became animated and altogether too loud for Richard's taste. He launched into another tirade.

'Not a clone, but something far worse – someone who looks at you and somehow knows the very essence of your being. Right down to your most intimate thoughts and fantasies. The things that you normally keep hidden from the world. Things that any normal person wouldn't care to know about themselves.'

Richard's curiosity was fuelled and he ordered another couple of brandies, trying to appear unruffled by what he had heard.

'Sounds rather dangerous. Certainly not the sort of person you'd give your home phone number to.'

Les was too drunk to be coherent, but he knew that Richard was condescending to him. It was pointless explaining. Richard was only a businessman trying to do a deal for his artist. There would be nothing gained by explaining that this evil spirit didn't need telephone numbers, it was already inside him. He offered to pay for the dinner with travellers' cheques, to bring it to an end. The idea of Les dutifully signing them in twenty-dollar portions was too much for Richard. He didn't want to be given a pauper's table the next time he went there. He would have paid anyway – he could claim it back on expenses.

Driving back, Richard reflected that the two would complement each other perfectly. It was his privately held view that artists were by definition insecure, and as long as he could tap into that insecurity, his position would be strong. Les was in the middle of a severe confidence crisis and would depend on Richard's calming influence. It was important for Les to think that he and Richard had a connection of some sort. For Les, the shirt, the fact that Hilditch and Key had supplied both men, would be enough. The shirt was classy and sober; it counteracted Les's view of a business that was flashy, tasteless and corrupt. From now on, as much as he liked his loafers from Bally and the slightly gaudy leisure shirts bought at the Polo Lounge of the Beverly Hills hotel, he made sure to wear sober attire from Savile Row and Kensington whenever he was due to meet Les. Well-cut, conservative sports jackets and pinstripe suits from the best tailors. He'd have it down to the last detail, even making sure he had a box of matches from the Savoy Grill or the Ritz. Les needed to be shown that his representative had the necessary panache to undertake business on his behalf. The one time Les had stalled, and refused to give him *carte blanche* in the negotiations, Richard had returned to his office to find that he was wearing an Armani shirt and a sweater from Pierre Cardin. The slight inconsistency had triggered off a deep insecurity in Les.

Most of the meetings, though, went well, and Les was greeted with warm interest. Richard stalled about the new material, but both knew Les would have to come up with some 'product' soon. Richard flew back to London, and Les took the Red-Eye to New York. He tried to write, but couldn't, and started to play some old tapes of demos from previous projects. Secret songs from his own archives that he would normally hide from the world. Perhaps they would work as a taster. Richard was right: when the deal was done, his inspiration would return and he would put the old songs back in his private collection.

The phone rang. Richard allowed himself to sound excited as he broke the news.

'The A and R department at United is really interested. They want to hear some songs. Then they can get started with the contract.'

Les lurched into insecurity. He had been in this situation before. He was flattered they wanted to sign him, but sceptical in case they just wanted proof he could still deliver. And deliver material that would suit *them*. Demos usually 'showed promise'. By the time it came round to making the real thing expectations would be raised so high nothing would sound good enough. They'd mix and over-dub his songs into oblivion. It had happened before. Songs should stay simple, and for demos, you needed skill and imagination to hear the quality through the crude hiss of the recording, the rough vocal and acoustic guitar or piano. The best producers could hear a germ of an idea, and knew how to take it forward. That was in an ideal world. In this world things were different. Value was judged by units sold. No one cared how the song had come to be written, the story behind every line, the emotions that drove that fragile first vocal. The record execs might make a song a hit, have it produced by some whizz kid, but as far as Les was concerned, that first homespun recording was as good as the track would ever get.

His songs acted as a form of diary, a soundtrack to his own life. Les wrote songs to try and make a connection inside himself, to chronicle his journeys from one part of his life to another. It was his passion as well as his job, and many of his songs never found their way into the recording studio. They were often the most personal. They ended up in notebooks or scribbled on the back of menus. Sometimes they just remained story outlines, sketches that might turn into something some day. The song was only an idea, an assembly of thoughts and images blended together with harmony and rhythm, with a beginning, middle and end. Every one was a part of him, of the half-invented person that he had become. The transient traveller, the disbeliever. A refugee searching for a place to fit in.

He looked through his catalogue of half-composed verses and cryptic notes. He'd collected all his lyrics to try and patch together his life, to link together the myriad twists and turns that built up both his creative and life experience. But in many ways he had just become more and more detached. It was almost as if he had lived two lives, one as the writer of the songs and one who inhabited the songs. None of it was made up. It was all real. And if the song was a deception, so was he. He needed to discover whether his life had been truly lived or merely conceptualized. To write new material, he needed to know who he was, and then abandon himself. He turned to another lyric. Or was it a new chapter in his life? He read the words but hardly recognized them as being his.

> Like a seed that is sown
> All the children are scattered,
> By a breeze that is blown
> Now the crops are all scattered.
> We are torn, we are tattered
> And some of us are barmy and battered.
> And the fields where we gathered
> Are overgrown with weeds that are scattered.
> Through it all, we were scattered . . .
>
> Now my life is all scattered
> Ever since she's been gone
> I feel older, I feel fatter
> I feel the blues coming on . . .
>
> We get bruised, we get battered
> But we'll pick up the pieces that
> Scattered and with emotional glue
> We're gonna stick together body and mind.

He'd written it after coming out of that dark period he had tried to explain to Richard over dinner. A time when his emotions had been tormented by that other evil spirit he claimed he had become obsessed by. Then, there had been the break-up of a marriage, followed by the death of his mother. Les had been in America when she died and had never quite got over the guilt at not being there. Who was the 'she' referred to in the lyric? Surely not his mum. And 'the fields where we gathered' was strange, because Les had grown up in the city. Maybe the song had helped him, but that didn't make it a hit. He put a tape of it into a cassette player and looked around in his closet to see if he had any others worth sending. The closet stank of old newspaper and dust. Almost like a tomb. Old photographs fell out of books and reminded Les of the way he had looked in 1966, then 1973. A framed poster advertising a college date in Poughkeepsie in the autumn of 84 fell on his head. In the other room 'Scattered' played, and put Les into emotional rewind. It could have been 1977.

Rock and Roll Fantasy

When the seasons change in New York, its inhabitants seem to celebrate more than any population on the planet. When events unify the collective conscious of the population, New York City seems like a small village. Only the outsiders, the lost people and the misfits, stand out. In every coffee shop and small bar, a little piece of the Manhattan jigsaw is acted out.

The celebrity photographs hanging on the wall of the Dakota diner on the Upper West Side were well known to the clientele. The comedian Henny Youngman gazed down fondly at the little old ladies who came into the diner for the two-dollar special. Milton Berle looked down compassionately as the Puerto Rican office boy carried out twenty-four assorted cups of coffee. The Dakota diner was on the ground floor of a sprawling, run-down old apartment block that once upon a time had jutted above the Manhattan skyline. Now, it lay in the shadow of newer buildings. The Dakota diner was a small-time café in big-time New York. The Carnegie or Stage delicatessen it wasn't. One look at the menu and you could see through its pretence; it was a Greek café masquerading as a chic Upper West Side coffee shop.

Christo, the overwrought owner, proudly displayed an auto-graphed photo of Elvis Presley, and he swore that the signature was authentic. The story went that in 1973 Elvis's limousine had pulled up outside, and he had walked in and ordered a deluxe cheeseburger and a chocolate milkshake to go. Christo had asked for a signed photograph, and two or three weeks later the picture had arrived:

'To Christo. Many thanks. Your old friend, Elvis.' Other celebs had come into the diner, but no one as big as Elvis. There was nothing special about the place. There were thousands like it in New York.

On this particular day, Danny, a downcast-looking fellow, carrying a large satchel full of autograph books and rock albums, walked past the diner two or three times before going in. He was one of the regulars, but for some reason he hesitated. Christo sighed. He knew the reason.

Danny was either short and fat or tall and thin depending on how life was treating him. Today he was unshaven and had dark rings under his eyes, as if he hadn't slept. Hunched up, his mind in turmoil. This was Danny on a good day – an old-looking twenty-eight, depending on the light. On a bad day, a young-looking forty.

Danny finally decided to go in, and took a good hard look at Christo. Christo's days of rock and roll were over. Surely he could never have danced to it. He could just about buy the notion of Milton Berle or Henny Youngman sending Christo an autographed picture, but Danny, a collector himself, remained sceptical about the signature on the photo of the King. OK, the Dakota diner was on the fashionable Upper West Side, spitting distance from Central Park West, near the Dakota building where John Lennon lived with Yoko Ono. Sure, Shelley Winters could sometimes be seen walking her poodles along the street. True, you could see Mia Farrow wheeling a baby in a pushchair along outside the Dakota building, and yes, everybody knew that once Paul Simon had sat in the corner having eggs over easy with his attorney, but Elvis Presley walking up to Christo to order a deluxe cheeseburger during a busy lunch hour? Unlikely.

Christo cringed when the Latino water boy shouted across the café.

'Here comes Danny, the wacko rock and roll fan.'

Danny flashed his discoloured teeth and looked over at the water boy threateningly. Christo tried to defuse the heat of the moment.

'Let's face it, Danny, you've got to be a wacko to be that passionate about rock music.'

Danny gritted his teeth and took a deep breath, then sat in his usual seat at the counter and gave the water boy that I'll-deal-with-you-later look. Danny had been a rock fan ever since he had seen Elvis on the Ed Sullivan show. He had moved across the Brooklyn Bridge into Manhattan to work in a small record store six blocks away, just off Broadway and Amsterdam – a big step from the working-class neighbourhood he had grown up in. It was a small store that catered mainly for record collectors and specialists. Danny was a real expert. An *aficionado* of the twelve-inch album and a collector of seven-inch singles, he had an encyclopaedic knowledge of every record released, every artist. Scrapbooks full of signatures. Letters from all over the world, from the international network of rock and roll fans. Danny had always been a bit of a loner, but when he became an adult he became even more isolated when all his friends got steady jobs, married, and forgot about rock music. For Danny, rock music was his life. Everything revolved around music and record magazines. The move from Brooklyn was inevitable once he heard that John Lennon had bought that apartment. All Danny's friends were still in Brooklyn, and whenever he went back to visit he would spin yarns about how well he was doing in Manhattan. The record business was on the up. Sales were at an all-time high. But today, Danny looked like he was on a short fuse. He looked like a vagrant. Over the edge. All hope gone. Desperate.

'Paulette isn't coming back.'

Christo cleaned the counter and said nothing. The old lady looked up from her two-dollar special. Danny continued, even though nobody really wanted to hear about it.

'She's gonna get married. It was on the radio for Christ's sake. She's marrying the rock singer.'

Christo felt he had to say something, even though he had heard the saga a hundred times before.

'The guy in the heavy metal band?'

Danny considered this to be a major humiliation.

'That's right. It'll be all over the city. Everyone will know. It'll probably be in the music trades. They were seen coming out of Studio 54. What will I do? What will I say to my friends? My folks?'

Christo slid over a glass of ice water. Danny was still talking away.

'To think. I asked her to marry me. I told everyone. We were as good as engaged. The humiliation!'

Christo put a menu in front of Danny and tried to commiserate.

'These things happen, you know. Maybe it's a flash in the pan. The rock singer will find somebody else and pretty soon she'll be back. Hey! Do you want the special or what?'

Danny was in no mood to be humoured.

'She returned my vintage Vic Damone collection. It's over between us.'

Christo shrugged. He knew the score. Paulette was a pretty, if somewhat stupid, nineteen-year-old from New Jersey, who worked in a boutique on Columbus Avenue. She wore thick, bright rock and roll make-up, and her big, black wire-like hair was piled up on top of her head. Her body was straight off the centrefold of *Hustler*. Neat tush, just about covered by a leather mini skirt, and tits like melons. One day she had walked into Danny's store looking for an obscure Aerosmith album, and once they had started talking, and she had looked at him with her big brown eyes, he knew that she was the one for him. To Danny it was all too psychic. Her name was the title of an Everly Brothers B-side. They were meant for each other. He'd never thought to ask if she felt the same way. Paulette was a trophy he could take home to Brooklyn and show his friends. He had spent all he had on her. He took her to the Copacabana on a date. To a ball game at Shea Stadium, where he bored her with stories about when the Beatles had played there. Danny had borrowed money to treat Paulette and, eventually, people came to collect. Christo had taken pity and offered him work in the kitchen to earn extra cash. Paulette never moved in with Danny, but he called her 'his girl' and treated her like a goddess. After she had endured the relationship for six months, Danny was still looking for new ways to impress her, anything so she would stay with him. He pandered to her every whim. One night, he took her backstage after a heavy metal concert, and she ran off with the singer. Now that she had gone off with him for good, he was devastated, a wreck. Danny was in love with her. He kept calling her, leaving messages, asking her to come back. Offering any albums she wanted, just as long as she'd return. Talking about her constantly. It had been a month now.

'Listen, Danny. You know you're better off without her. You know when guys looked at her it always put you on edge. Why are you still carrying a torch for this broad?'

Danny wouldn't stop talking about her. She didn't return his calls. He'd gone to her parents' house in Yonkers to find her. They'd thrown him out, and got a restraining order. Christo just shook his head and put a bowl of soup in front of Danny.

'It's barley today. Do me a favour, Danny. Get yourself a life. Forget her.'

This hit a chord with Danny.

'That's what Paulette's dad said. He told me to get a life. Said rock music wasn't life.'

He ate, and carried on talking. The landlord at his apartment had served an eviction notice. It was only a tiny room, but the Upper West Side was out of Danny's league. Christo tried to cheer him up.

'I don't know why you keep that apartment. You spend all your time here, at work, or hanging around at rock concerts. Sub-let it.'

Christo wasn't wrong. The few people that had seen Danny's

apartment said it was nothing more than a storeroom for all his records and memorabilia. And not big enough a storeroom either. Danny continued to complain.

'It's a real struggle. The music industry may be on the up, but in the city, everybody's broke. You have to be a millionaire to live in this city.'

Christo was in philosophical mode. He had his own problems. The Dakota diner had seen better times. Each day he'd try another scam, another cheap combo to entice customers in.

'Tell me about it. I'm not looking for millionaires. Just regular poor folks would be fine, as long as they can pay for a two-dollar special.'

He started looking through the albums in Danny's satchel.

'This record collection must be worth something. If you sold it, you'd make a fortune.'

Danny got protective and closed the bag.

'Don't worry about me. I'm fine. I'll die before I sell my record collection.'

Christo knew when to stop. Danny didn't like talking about money. Music was all that mattered. But it made him less than a person. He was a collector, a dealer in trivia. He neglected himself, his own life; his collection, and Paulette, were his only source of pride. Even the daily ritual of going to the diner at lunchtime was not to feed himself, but to feed his obsession with music and Paulette, by talking, talking, talking. Christo looked out on to the street.

'This used to be a neighbourhood. Working people. Small stores. Now the businessmen are moving in. Boutiques everywhere. Smart restaurants, with fancy décor. Nobody likes plain food any more. You can't have a conversation with anybody. Nobody has the time.'

Danny just nodded his head.

'That's why I have music. Without that, I couldn't hang on. When Paulette and I used to quarrel I'd go home and put on "Can't Buy Me Love". That got me through some difficult times.'

And when his eldest brother had gone off to Vietnam and never came back, he had played his old Frank Zappa albums day in, day out. Somehow Danny felt there was some of his brother left on those albums.

Christo hadn't known Danny very long, but he was easy to read. Danny was hanging tough right now, but the tell-tale signs were there. He was heading for a slump, beginning to neglect himself more than usual. Some lunchtimes he didn't even come in — a sure sign self-pity had set in. He'd gone missing before, and Christo would receive a postcard from Memphis or some such place. Danny had been to visit Graceland, a pilgrimage in his time of despair. Christo was getting used to it. Danny was always doing crazy things. Once he hitchhiked upstate to Rochester because two of the Jimi Hendrix Experience were playing a club date. On the way back, he had been mugged and had all of his money taken. They even took a few albums. He'd hustled a pass into the club, though. Christo wondered what would pick him up this time.

Danny finished his soup and walked out of the diner, but instead of going back to the record store, he walked around the Upper West Side, revisiting all the places he had taken Paulette. He walked past the Ansonia building on Broadway and 71st, a large, sprawling, once glamorous hotel, which was now being converted into apartments. Paulette did keep-fit on the second floor, and Danny used to wait for her there. Then there was the Genoa Italian restaurant opposite the subway station at 72nd where he took her on their first date. He walked around the neighbourhood until the restaurants had closed and the chefs piled the wasted food on the street, ready for the refuse collection the following morning. Danny looked at a dog foraging through the garbage and remembered how he and Paulette used to laugh at the dogs and their owners leading them around the Upper West Side. They'd wondered how so many large dogs could live in so many small apartments. Then, standing outside the Lincoln Center, he decided he had to get her back. The following day he talked to Christo again.

'She always loved breakfast on the West Side. Sunday brunch up the road at Ruskay's, she can't refuse.'

Danny was optimistic, Christo a realist.

'There's no way she'll come. It's too late.'

Danny wouldn't listen, and started writing the letter. Paulette had loved walking along Columbus Avenue on a Sunday morning. Danny had *The New York Times* under his arm. He never read it, but it made him feel like a real New Yorker. They would stroll up to Ruskay's, stand in line until a table was free. The stares hadn't started getting to him yet. As long as she went home with him, that's all he cared about. If she read the letter and met him one more time at Ruskay's, he could convince her that she was making a big mistake. The dream of a last-ditch reconciliation gave Danny new hope, but Christo knew his Brooklyn friend was grasping at a thread. Danny messengered the letter over express.

Sunday morning came, and Danny was up at the crack of dawn, showered and sparkling and ready to meet Paulette. He'd bought a new tie-dyed T-shirt, and checked out his new look with Christo.

'Not bad,' said the Greek. 'You look too classy for this place. Get out of here.'

Danny smiled and swaggered cockily out of the diner. The satchel full of albums over his shoulder made him lurch. Across the street he saw a familiar face. Lester Mulligan was walking into the hotel opposite. Danny was in two minds. Paulette wouldn't be at Ruskay's for at least half an hour. Surely there'd be time to get his autograph. He went over and hassled the doorman for information.

'Is Mr Mulligan moving into the neighbourhood? Is he just visiting?'

The doorman tried to say nothing, but eventually gave in to Danny's persistence.

'Yes. Mr Mulligan is staying in New York for a while to write some songs. Now get lost, will ya?'

Danny bought a coffee and sat in the street until he saw Les Mulligan come out. Then he rushed over and bombarded him with questions, treating him like an old friend, showing his press clippings, talking non-stop.

'It's such a trip to think that you and John Lennon are gonna be next-door neighbours. It's too far out.'

The singer was not so enthusiastic.

'Yeah, I guess everybody's got to live somewhere.'

Danny was over-excited, over-inquisitive. Overstepping the boundaries.

'You must get together a lot with John and Yoko. Do you still fight with your band? I guess John can relate because of the way he quarrelled with Paul. You sure must have a lot to talk about.' Danny started to drool.

The rock singer smiled and promised to leave a photograph of his band with the doorman. Danny stood and watched Lester Mulligan walk towards Central Park. A limousine pulled up outside the Dakota building. Danny couldn't believe his luck as he saw John Lennon walk out and get in. Two of his idols in the space of five minutes, and on the same street. It was more than he could have hoped for. It had to be a good omen. He'd get back with Paulette. He hung around the limo as Lennon signed autographs for a couple of giggling girls. Danny was talking again, showing off his insider knowledge.

'I hear that you and the other Beatles are going to get together again to make another album?'

John Lennon looked over.

'Not in the foreseeable future, I shouldn't think. I've got my own solo project. That takes up all of my time.'

Danny jumped in with another question.

'Are you aware of the Shea Stadium bootleg album? We had a

couple in the store where I work, but when my boss found out they were bootlegs he refused to sell them. Just thought you ought to know that, John.'

He'd hit a nerve. John looked hard at Danny, and cast it off, saying that Shea Stadium was a long time ago and that nobody really cared any more. He mumbled a few more inaudible sentences before getting into the limousine and driving off down Central Park West.

Danny ran down to the newspaper stand by the subway station at Columbus Avenue and bought a *New York Times* as a talisman. He was in Ruskay's in time to claim a decent table where he could sit and watch the street. Hours seemed to pass. Danny flicked through the paper and reluctantly ordered brunch for one: eggs over easy, jelly, cheesecake, coffee. After six refills, it was obvious that Paulette wasn't coming. Maybe she hadn't got the letter, maybe she had. The waiter told Danny they needed the table. Danny left, but walked up and down the street, hoping she'd just been delayed. He felt like one of those sad dogs tied up outside, waiting for their owners to come and reclaim them. The streets were getting crowded, the Upper West Side was starting to buzz. So many people. But for Danny, without Paulette, it was the loneliest place on earth.

He found himself back in his apartment, surrounded by rent demands and his memorabilia. He started to write a suicide letter. He blamed his parents, his poor start in Brooklyn. He even lost faith in his music. She had been driven away by his obsession. He blamed anything, any excuse to mask the simple reality that Paulette just didn't love him any more. Perhaps she never had. Danny put the note in his wallet to carry around with him, just in case he could summon up the courage to end it all.

Days went past. Danny walked around, unwashed, existing in a blurred, meaningless world. He had lost his job at the record store. He had stopped going to the Dakota diner. It had grown cold. Last winter he hadn't noticed it. The cold air had only made him anticipate being in a warm bed with Paulette. People didn't seem to smile. He was alone, and the cold was just an accompaniment to his empty life. He still had the suicide letter in his wallet. Every day he thought of death. He'd left his love records to Paulette. Even in death he could serenade her through the voices of Paul McCartney, Roy Orbison and Elvis. 'Yesterday', 'Only the Lonely' and 'Are You Lonesome Tonight?' would be the epitaph to his love for Paulette. Maybe he was only now living in the real world. There was no place for him in it.

Christo would look out for Danny on the street. He could see only the black panhandler in his usual spot outside the Olcott Hotel. The dry chill of winter had pushed out the warm air of fall. The hot air belching out of the vent where the panhandler stood would give him some relief, at least. Christo could shift a lot of soup.

The seasons came and went. Danny took any work going, washing up in restaurants, walking dogs for little old ladies on the West Side. Anything to help take his mind off Paulette and his humiliation. One day he even walked past Lester Mulligan as he jogged through Central Park. He'd shouted out to Danny, but he had been too depressed to answer back, too ashamed to say that he had rejected the music he once loved. He had set the time for his death. The day was fixed in his mind, circled on the calendar. On 16 August his alarm clicked on as usual at 7.30 a.m. It was his and Paulette's anniversary. Today he wasn't going to shift himself from his bed. Today was the day when somebody would finally get to read his suicide note. He flicked around the dial on the radio and settled on WNEW to listen to rock and roll for the last time. Then a reporter cut into a track to give the world the news from Memphis, Tennessee.

Elvis Presley had been found dead at his home at Graceland. Listeners were advised to stay tuned for further updates. Danny stayed by the radio to hear the details as they emerged. The sound of the announcer's voice echoed deep inside his head. The King

31

was dead. Rock and roll had crashed into the real world, and Danny's world had been stopped dead in its tracks. His own death would have to be delayed. He spent all day and night tuned into various rock stations for the latest news. He started to wonder how Christo would deal with it. It didn't seem to matter now whether or not the autograph was authentic. That wasn't important. It was the fact that Christo believed it was that mattered. For once Paulette didn't fill his mind. His problems were minuscule compared to facing a world without Elvis. He wrote her a kiss-off note, a final goodbye. He was going back to Brooklyn to be with real people, people he knew and trusted. Then suddenly, amidst the tributes, he spotted that one of the DJs was playing a stereo remix of 'It's Alright, Mama' instead of the original mono mix. He looked through his collection for the original, and his taste for music came back.

That night Danny couldn't sleep. At three in the morning he looked up at the large hotel building where Lester Mulligan had been staying and saw a light in one of the windows. He fantasized that it was Mulligan, still up listening to the radio for news about Elvis.

'Yeah,' Danny thought. 'He must be a fan too. I guess he can't sleep either.'

■

Hallo you, hallo me, hallo people we used to be,
Isn't it strange, we never change, we've been through it all yet
   we're still the same,
And I know it's a miracle we still go,
For all we know we might still have a way to go.

Hallo me, hallo you, you say you want out, want to start anew,
Throw in your hand, break up the band, start a new life, be a new man,
But for all we know we might still have a way to go,
Before you go there's something you ought to know.

ROCK AND ROLL FANTASY

There's a guy in my block, he lives for rock, he plays records day
    and night,
And when he feels down he puts some rock and roll on and it
    makes him feel all right,
And when he feels the world is closing in, he turns the stereo way
    up high,
He just spends his life living in a rock and roll fantasy,
He just spends his life living on the edge of reality,
He just spends his life in a rock and roll fantasy.

Look at me, look at you, you say we've got nothing left to prove,
The King is dead, rock is done, you might be through but I've
    just begun,
I don't know, I feel free and I won't let go,
Before you go there's something you ought to know.

Dan is a fan and he lives for our music, it's the only thing that gets
    him by,
He's watched us grow and he's seen all our shows, he's seen us
    low and he's seen us high,
Oh but you and me keep thinking that the world's just passing us
    by,
Don't want to spend my life living in a rock and roll fantasy,
Don't want to spend my life living on the edge of reality,
Don't want to waste my life hiding away any more.

Don't want to spend my life living in a rock and roll fantasy.

Mr Pleasant

Matthew R. Ellis was a senior consultant in the firm of Sullivan, Barr & Jewelson, a well-respected firm of City accountants. Every aspect of his life had been meticulously planned, and reaching middle life held no fears for him. All arrangements had been made. The pension was in order; the mortgage fully paid up. A healthy surplus in the bank gave him immunity from any tax-grabbing political party or fluctuation on the stock exchange. His position in the world was assured, and his confidence knew no limitations. He had reached the pinnacle of his profession, and his ebullience, tempered with moderation, ensured his longevity and success. In many ways Ellis was untouchable.

The commute from Huntingdon to London was eased by travelling outside rush hour. Those years were over. He had even considered selling off his Barbican *pied-à-terre* and retiring early to a small house in the south of France. As he sat back in the comfort of his first-class carriage he pondered on a life arranged and accounted for with slide-rule precision. He felt confident about his future, and with good reason. His life had indeed been a success. Corporate accountancy had served him well. The fact that his children had always thought him a grey, dull, uninteresting man did not bother him in the slightest. Restraint had been a key factor in his life. He had watched so many businessmen fall by the wayside over the years because of their inability to plan through a recession or trim the excess, to reduce, scale down, downsize. Some friends and relatives thought that M.R. had been much too cautious. He could have entered politics had he taken the chance, but failure was too much of a gamble. His middle name was Ralph but he always joked that the R stood for Respectability.

To be thought of as respectable was all he ever wanted; to have a career, all that he ever wished. So why was he now sitting in the waiting room at Sullivan, Barr & Jewelson, feeling insecure for the first time in his adult life? He looked over at the ticking clock which had been hanging on the wall when he first came to the company as a young trainee bookkeeper nearly half a century earlier. Its iron hands had been punctual all that time. It showed 10.25. He was five minutes early. As he sat in the deathly silence he wondered why he had been called, so suddenly, in this cloak-and-dagger way. Who would be his inquisitor? What questions would he ask? Surely he could not be implicated in any wrongdoing? His tracks were always well covered. Waiting for the hands to tick to 10.30 his emotions churned over inside him. Fear. Horror of the unknown. In his mind he mulled over his latest set of accounts to see if any errors had gone unnoticed. It was almost unthinkable for a man of his position to be in this situation, having his figures questioned, put to the test, his professionalism on the line. If anything were discovered his credibility would be in question, and as his whole profession was founded on trust, it could mean ruin.

Ellis had most recently been in contact with the Inland Revenue about the dealings of a limited company that had been attracting the Inspector's eye. A garment company Ellis had helped set up in the late 1970s. The company director was a get-rich-quick merchant, a self-made man, whose company had expanded under Thatcherism and had been well on the way to becoming a public company before the 1988 recession hit. Unfortunately, the director had developed the habit of questioning every bill sent in and claiming expenses that were not fully substantiated in the company accounts. It was all terribly untidy and really should have been dealt with by one of the junior staff, but the company director, a stubborn working-class lout, had been ringing up Ellis's office constantly, demanding personal attention. When Ellis tried to explain that his fees as a consultant were way above the means of the company, the director had specified that the main requirement for settling fees outstanding was that Ellis himself undertook the work. This behaviour would have been tolerated in the 1960s, and even in bullish Thatcher's Britain, where anything was possible if the fees were paid up. But now, in the more cautious era of the late 1980s, people were drifting back to where they were before the swinging sixties encouraged the classes to mingle unrestrainedly. Any spiv or barrow boy finding himself with enough profit had been able to invest in a mansion in the home counties, join the landed gentry, send his children to the best schools and, worse still, have these lowly offspring enter the professions. They had encroached on Ellis's middle-class peers and were ultimately responsible for the gradual decline in the standards of the medical, legal and accountancy professions. Ellis had seen the writing on the wall for the get-rich-quick merchant's company and had decided to refer it to the Inspector, and save his own reputation.

For the next few years Ellis lay the groundwork for the demise of the company. The books were primed with little inconsistencies that to an uninformed eye seemed innocuous enough. There was nothing illegal in what Ellis was doing, in fact he went to great lengths to ensure that every company account was authorized by the company director and that every account submitted to the Inspector included Ellis's disclaimer, 'on the information supplied to us'. Recently, an insolvency practitioner had been consulted, and the company director was running scared, chasing his tail trying to stop the company from going under. It would only be a matter of time before the Revenue made its move and the situation would come to a comfortably satisfying end. This would not be before Ellis's bills had been settled. He had broken the golden rule and doctored his time sheets to justify his fees. When, as anticipated, the company director complained, Ellis made the grand gesture of accepting slightly less for an immediate settlement. The company director thought he had beaten Ellis down, but the accountant still received his standard rate. Everybody was satisfied. Even so, Ellis knew the company couldn't afford it. Nevertheless, this wearisome exercise of securing fees was dealt with, and the rest would be up to the bankruptcy courts. Nobody at Sullivan, Barr & Jewelson would ever suspect a trusted associate such as M. R. Ellis of fiddling his books. In fact, Ellis took great pride in knowing that he had helped rid the business world of a scurrilous maverick, that he had struck a blow for the middle classes and put another upstart opportunist back in his place. It wasn't considered illegal and was becoming customary procedure in the City. Ellis was simply securing his fees. Surely such a normal, everyday bankruptcy wasn't the reason for Ellis being summoned to this meeting? Ellis had laid the bait. The predators would be waiting, and M. R. Ellis could go his happy way, with a pleasant smile on his face.

Messrs Sullivan, Barr & Jewelson had all died long ago. They would have remembered young M. R. Ellis starting at the firm. A keen and trustworthy young bookkeeper. They would have vouched for his reliability. For his impeccable record and devoted service to the company. Jewelson's grandson ran the company now, and he hated M. R. Ellis's guts. Jewelson the younger had tried to streamline the company, to bring it into the eighties, maximize profits and go global. In Jewelson's book, M.R. was a dinosaur. A relic from an age when accountants were not considered businessmen. A time when professions were cherished, trustworthy, unassailable. Now the bottom line was all important and Jewelson Jr, or J.J. as the young secretaries called him, was intent on dragging this tired old accountancy firm into the twentieth century. M. R. Ellis sat looking at the clock. It was 10.50. What could be holding them up? Every so often a secretary would walk out of the boardroom. She would say 'Good morning, Mr Ellis,' courteously, almost as if she knew something she was afraid to tell him. At 11.15 Jewelson Jr's young female assistant emerged.

'Mr Jewelson apologizes for the delay, Mr Ellis, but he wonders if the meeting could be scheduled for three o'clock this afternoon after the corporate lunch.'

Ellis's suspicions were confirmed. A pain shot up the right side of his jaw, the tension was getting to him. He was well aware of corporate moves, and this was a bad sign. It was unprecedented that such a senior employee should be kept waiting in this way. Something was definitely up. He tried to make light of the matter, saying that was perfect and fitted in with his plans. It would be a chance for him to do some shopping in the West End. He had a lunch appointment at Claridge's with an old friend but would do his best to get back by three o'clock.

M. R. Ellis could have waited in his office, but that would have been too humiliating. The Board was having lunch sent in, and it would have been obvious that he had stayed in the building. The corporate cars were waiting outside for the other directors and members of the Board but Ellis knew too well that these empty limousines would not be available to him, so he hailed a cab to take him into the West End. He thought about going to Fortnum & Mason for a light lunch, but instead he got out of the taxi cab at Trafalgar Square. For some reason Regent Street seemed too crowded, so he wandered down past Piccadilly Circus, up Beak Street, and ended up in a little café next to a striptease club. He would be safe there. Nobody he knew would be there. He felt invisible. Someone would have recognized him at Fortnum's or Claridge's. Questions would have been asked, and M. R. Ellis was in no mood to answer.

'What could possibly be wrong?' Ellis thought. Perhaps when he eventually met with the partners he would receive a golden handshake and that would be it. But if criminal activity was involved, they might strip him of all his benefits and ceremonially dismiss him from the firm. He would be an outcast in the only profession he had known in his life. And all because he tried to do the right thing. This could be the worst day of his life.

After ordering a light lunch in the café, Ellis watched as various disreputable characters sauntered in and out of the stripclub next door. Most seemed like regular clients, but some could be seen entering another door to the side of the main entrance. Ellis deduced that it must have led to a brothel of some description, where businessmen and executives could indulge in a little lunch-time shenanigans. The club did not look unlike one he had gone to when he first qualified as an accountant. His chums had dragged him along on a drunken night on the town, and Ellis had been propositioned by numerous women before accepting the services of a large black dominatrix. A spurt of youth before entering the hallowed halls. As Ellis ordered an expresso from a squat Italian waitress, he cast his mind back fondly to that humiliating encounter. He was drifting into lurid recollections of whips and anal tormentors when the mobile phone in his briefcase started ringing. The secretary on the other end of the line sounded harassed.

'Sorry to interrupt your lunch, Mr Ellis, but Mr Jewelson has been called to West End Central for an interview with the police. Could the meeting be put back until five this afternoon?'

M.R.'s heart was beating heavily, but his experience told him to remain calm and aloof. He weighed up his options carefully. Making sure the secretary heard his irritated sigh, he slowly re-sponded.

'Oh dear, how inconvenient. I'll have to move some things around; my secretary is not with me but I'm sure something can be done. Yes, I will do my best to get there.'

Ellis clicked the off switch before the secretary could say goodbye. As he put the phone back in his briefcase, he could see that his hands were shaking and he took his handkerchief out of his top jacket pocket to wipe the sweat off his palms.

'West End Central,' Ellis thought. 'What next? The serious fraud squad?'

His head was starting to throb and his mind accelerated. He tried to think back to any other impropriety in his past. Any figures and facts that could be construed as in any way criminal. Any tracks left uncovered or mistakes made. At that moment a woman wearing sunglasses, her face caked with bright-coloured make-up, walked in from the stripclub and ordered a cup of tea. She sat down opposite him and smiled. At first, Ellis was slightly agitated by her intrusion but then felt a little relieved by her presence, and while she would never see fifty again, there was a certain cheap coquettishness about her, the allure that she would still submit to depravity for the right price. Ellis smiled at her in a kind, benevolent way as she swigged her tea, and imagined putting the slag's tongue to good use. Then he checked his watch. 2.49. The woman returned Ellis's smile, as if she had suddenly spotted him as potential trade. The thought had crossed his mind. If his day would end in a prison cell, why not enjoy what was left of it? There would be nothing gained by phoning his wife now. She would burst into tears and he would have to spend the rest of the day consoling her. In any event, she would have ample opportunity to visit him in prison. Then it struck him. Prison. How unsavoury. How utterly sad. It would be too much for his poor wife to take. The magnitude of the disgrace would force her to move from their comfortable mansion in Huntingdonshire to more modest quarters in Southgate or Hackney. His ignominious demise would be splashed across the front page of the *Financial Times* for his friends to gloat over while they sank the nineteenth hole at the golf club. He remembered the threat made by the director of the garment business when Ellis had explained that after discussions with the Revenue, there was no alternative but to put the company into liquidation.

'If I go down, I'll take you and your kind with me.'

Perhaps the little snitch had implicated Ellis and the whole firm was in jeopardy. That was possibly why Jewelson had to go to the police, to answer allegations. The woman was still looking at Ellis. He thought about asking how much, as if that was a problem. At that moment in time M. R. Ellis could afford anything he wanted. 'Nessun Dorma' was reaching its peak on the café stereo system and Ellis blurted it out.

'What do you do?'

The woman smiled back-like she had a customer on the hook. Then her face broke into that Strictly Business grimace that Ellis appreciated. Her voice was quiet, but she pronounced each word clearly.

'Blow job, buggery, slavery, bondage, you name it, and for the right price I'll do anything you want.' She smiled and took another sip of tea.

Ellis arrogantly sipped his expresso and looked unimpressed. The woman leaned across the table and whispered in his face, almost threateningly.

'I'll bury you solid, you dirty old bastard, and your dick will be so hard they'll be able to lift you into the coffin by it with a crane.'

Ellis retained his composure, pouted, and politely put the cup of expresso down. The woman leaned back and smiled.

'But right now, I suggest you keep your money. Unless you're a gambling man.' The woman gestured towards two large thugs standing very conspicuously outside a porn shop. 'Those men are plain-clothes coppers and they've been watching the place for a few days now, but if we hurry up and you want to take the risk – well, what's life without risk?'

Ellis felt his mouth go dry. The woman had stirred some unsavoury thoughts in him and for the first time that day he started to forget about his fate at the hands of Sullivan, Barr & Jewelson. If he was going to go down, why not go down in style? He was just on the verge of accepting whatever discipline the woman imposed when his mobile phone rang again. He smiled politely at the woman as he reached into his briefcase. He tried to sound as sexy as possible but his voice cracked as he asked who was on the line. It was the secretary from the office.

'Sorry to interrupt you again, Mr Ellis, but the meeting with Mr Jewelson will have to be postponed.' Her voice broke at this point. Ellis looked into the eyes of the woman opposite. The distraught secretary spoke in a slow, tearful monotone.

'Mr Jewelson's daughter Amanda. She's been found dead. The police say it's murder. She was found on a piece of waste ground near the railway at Earlsfield. Mr Jewelson has gone to identify the body. Poor Amanda. Seventeen years old.'

For an instant Ellis could feel only relief and had to force himself to sound shocked, but his desperation returned.

'And the agenda. There was an agenda for the meeting?'

The secretary was too distressed to observe company protocol and revealed that some preparatory notes were still laid out for the other partners in the boardroom. Ellis saw his opportunity.

'I'll be in to collect a copy. It will help poor Mr Jewelson to know that other members of the company are covering for him in his desperate time of grief.' He quickly pressed the end-call button on his mobile and thrust it back into his briefcase. As he paid his bill, he noticed that the woman had left the cafeteria. Perhaps she had gone back into the stripclub to wait for him. If that was the case, she would have to wait for quite a while. Ellis had to see that agenda.

He left the café and looked around frantically for a taxi, but they all seemed to be taken. He thought of going by Tube, but as he started to walk down the steps of Leicester Square station, a gust of air from below almost blew him off his feet. He looked down into the steep descent which stretched almost to hell itself. He shuddered, and thought he heard a young girl crying out for help from the dark cavern below. The subway stank of death. He stepped back from the entrance, clutching his briefcase so hard his knuckles locked. A taxi turned the corner and Ellis rammed himself into the back seat, grateful and relieved. Now – composure. The journey was long enough for him to regain his poise.

But his mind wouldn't stop. That slightly devious tax pension scam in the Cayman Islands in the early seventies, surely that wasn't coming back to haunt him? The Revenue was callous at times, but at the end of the day, it always looked after its own. That was the way the establishment worked. It had a tidy way of dealing with anyone who drifted from the path, leaving them some standing in society when the rest of the world had forgotten their wrongdoings. There was the occasional share transaction that was a little irregular, but insider trading was something now dead and buried by Maxwell and the Lloyds débâcle. A purely cosmetic exercise in self-purgation to show the outside world that even the City was not above slapping itself on the wrist from time to time. Dishonesty still existed, but everyone turned a blind eye provided they didn't get burned themselves. But, sometimes, an example had to be made. A sacrifice to show the world that standards were being maintained and the professions were still squeaky clean. If that were the case, M.R. could do nothing. There would be no one to turn to. The true horror hit him: Surely no one could have traced him back to his modest upbringing above a cobbler's in a small Norfolk fishing town? That would be more crushing than any other exposé. It turned M.R.'s stomach. Ellis rose to the ranks when upbringing and social background were vital, even more important than ability to read a profit-and-loss account. He'd had to lie about his origins. It was true he had been educated at Cambridge, but at the grammar school and an evening institute rather than the university. He said he'd played rugby, but had actually only bought a scarf with the colours of the Varsity team. Elocution lessons had rid him of his rural accent and gained him the Queen's English. He'd joined the Norfolk Young Conservatives, and picked up some useful contacts, including membership of the local lawn-tennis club. The sham was further compounded when he married the daughter of a stockbroker and moved to Huntingdonshire. His family had not been invited to the wedding. He simply explained that his father had died and his mother was an eccentric locked away in an asylum. It was becoming easier and easier for Ellis to cover his tracks. His whole persona had been created for his new position in the world, and the irony was that while his chosen profession demanded a vow of honesty, his whole life was based on a falsehood. Now it was time for him to turn his back on the past and leap head-first into Middle England, become a respected member of the community and embrace the ruling classes. They thought of him as a thoroughly pleasant chap. Anyone from his own background was to be avoided at all costs.

As the taxi turned the corner of Threadneedle Street, M.R. approached the offices of Sullivan, Barr & Jewelson as if for the last time. He was now resigned to the fact that he would be a sacrifice, to preserve the status quo. It was better than being brought to heel by that little guttersnipe from the garment factory. In years to come the name of M. R. Ellis might even be up there with other martyrs for their class. In more noble times he would have had the choice of a bullet or a cyanide pill.

The door opened and Jewelson's secretary came towards him. She was sobbing into a handkerchief. Ellis could see that the board-room was empty. He told the distraught secretary to sit down and compose herself. She was holding some documents. Did they contain the details of his wrongdoings? If so, he would offer his resignation immediately.

M.R. almost grabbed the papers out of the secretary's hands. He glanced quickly through the agenda. Only a few minor decisions on a plan to extend the offices and the usual staff-holiday roster, plus a few other minor points of no particular interest. He breathed a sigh of relief. The large clock struck five and suddenly M. R. Ellis was composed and in control. He asked the secretary to pass on his condolences to Mr Jewelson, and after collecting some mail from his desk, he left work for the day.

Ellis made his way on to the platform at King's Cross just as the station clock rolled over to 5.30. His timing was perfect. He would be home on time, his wife would be none the wiser, he would console her after breaking the tragic news of Jewelson's daughter, go to bed, and sleep the sleep of a man reprieved. Taking a seat in the first-class compartment, he glanced down at the *Evening Standard* to see a report of a young woman's body found in the undergrowth near some railway tracks at Earlsfield, South London, and of a murder enquiry being launched. In the Stop Press section was a short paragraph about a police raid in Soho and several arrests in connection with etcetera, etcetera. M.R. had barely started reading the closing prices on the stock exchange when the train jolted forward and started its journey.

A few commuters ran alongside the train. Ellis was never late and had no sympathy for the few stragglers who missed the departure. As the train emerged out of the vast canopy covering the platforms, he remembered a tune from a long time ago, with a mocking lyric about a pleasant man who led a perfect existence. In his youth, Ellis could bring himself to laugh whenever he heard the song ridiculing a life that had been overcautious and secretive. If he heard the song now, it would probably offend him. Even in the most perfect world there was a dark corner. He had become the very thing he once despised. The lyric, in all its innocence, didn't say that it was possible to flout respectability. That it could camouflage more sinister deeds. At that moment the evening sun burst through the window and a ray of light shot into Ellis' eyes, making him flinch. A tear ran down the side of his cheek. He took out a handkerchief to wipe it away then felt a lump in his throat. Before he knew what was happening to him, another tear, then another. He buried his head in his hands and made his way through the crowded carriage hoping that no one would see that he was starting to cry. He stood in the corridor and watched the city flash past. Why had he suddenly started to weep in such a vulgar way? Was it relief at not being found out? Or the sudden realization that he was unable to find any feeling for Jewelson or his daughter? All the years of pretence had rid him of any true emotion. In order to gain, something had to be lost, and in M. R. Ellis's case profiting from the world had bankrupted his soul. But there was no profit in tears. His composure regained, he made his way to a vacant seat and returned to the closing prices in the City.

Oh, Mister Pleasant, how is Missus Pleasant?
I hope the world is treating you right.
And your head's in the air,
And you're feeling so proud,
Cos you're such a success,
And the whole wide world is on your side, hey hey,
How are you today?
People say Mister Pleasant is good,
Mister Pleasant is kind,
Mister Pleasant's OK,
Mister Pleasant don't mind,
As long as Mister Pleasant's all right, hey hey,
How are you today?

How's your father, how's your mother, how's your sister and
    your brother?
How's your brand-new limousine, twenty-four-inch TV screen?
Guess you like prosperity more than you like poverty,
Life is easier, so much easier now.

Oh, Mister Pleasant,
How is Missus Pleasant?
Did you know she was running around with another young man?
And he's taking her out when you have to work late,

49

And it's not so pleasant after all, hey hey.
How are you today?
People say Mister Pleasant is good, Mister Pleasant is kind,
Mister Pleasant's OK, Mister Pleasant don't mind,
As long as Mister Pleasant's all right,
Hey hey, how are you today?

Celluloid Heroes

(Or is it only a tinted photograph?)

Scene 1. Hollywood. Noon.

Music. A slick jazz theme as we pan across an idyllic Los Angeles landscape. Palm trees, expensive-looking mansions nestled in the hills. Blue skies and sunshine. Pan over to the Hollywood sign which looks over LA. Pull back to reveal that it's only a photograph. Track back to show that the photo is on the wall of Zero's seedy diner on Hollywood Boulevard. The expensive-sounding jazz music falls away to a solitary, sad saxophone phrase. The diner is dimly lit; the main light source is the daylight outside. Camera follows a petite blonde waitress dressed in a cute pink outfit. She stops at ENGLISH*'s table. He has long dark hair, a lean face and is wearing a tight-fitting cowboy shirt underneath a hippie waistcoat. His face is in half-shadow, he looks a little dangerous. He is writing in a notepad. The* NARRATOR *speaks, fast, in an American accent.*

NARRATOR This is Tinseltown USA, where everybody looks like they're in the movies and anybody can be a movie star. Just look at this guy. His name is English.

Track around ENGLISH *as he writes in his notepad. While the* NARRATOR *speaks we move in on other faces in the diner. Typical casualties of Hollywood. Vagrants and down and outs.*

NARRATOR At least he says he's from England. He even talks with an English accent. That's until he loses his temper and the North Carolina drawl slips back.

ENGLISH *twitches. He tries to drink a glass of water but his hands won't stop shaking. The ice cubes rattle and he can barely get the glass to his mouth. When he isn't writing he looks wrecked.*

NARRATOR He's a little high right now. Looks like a cool candidate for a religious epic – set in an asylum. English always had a strange fix on reality.

ENGLISH *puts on a pair of rose-tinted hippie glasses and stares straight ahead. He smiles at nothing in particular. He seems more optimistic.*

NARRATOR He looks at life through a tinted camera lens, his actions are contrived for an imaginary audience seated somewhere at the back of his head. Skipped right over by intellect and common sense.

ENGLISH's *POV. Now the down and outs are all wearing make-up; their features are enhanced by flattering lighting. They look like stars.*

NARRATOR English's world is an idealized world of movies, TV, comic books, all programmed to have beginnings, middles and ends. A complete fantasy addict. A prime candidate for Tinseltown USA. He's no star, but he's playing his own movie, his own epic. He's his own writer and narrator.

Close-up of ENGLISH's *lips. He mouths the words as he writes. His hands tremble slightly.*

ENGLISH . . . his own epic . . . He's his own writer and narrator.

ENGLISH *smiles, satisfied, sips his coffee. He looks up. Music builds. Whip pan following his eyeline to* ROSA DIABLO *standing in the doorway, silhouetted by the daylight outside. Dramatic chords, a sexy saxophone phrase. Focus on* ROSA, *as she steps into a shaft of light that shoots dramatically across her face. She's a babe, a femme fatale, auburn hair down past her shoulders, brooding lips, vulnerable and evil. She sees* ENGLISH.

NARRATOR But this babe is trouble. Rosa Diablo. Cheerleader, college drop-out, waitress, porn actress, bottomless dancer at the Rat Trap Club on Sunset. But when the light is right and through English's tinted glasses, she's Lauren Bacall in *To Have and Have Not*. Look at that walk.

All the down and outs are in on the scene, her big entrance. Bette Davis sits in a booth waiting for her next fix. Jean Harlow takes Bacall's order and passes it to Zero Mostel, two eggs over easy. That's Harpo Marx just leaving. Grilled cheese on wholewheat to go, he picks up his violin and it's back to his pitch on the corner of Wilcox and Hollywood.

Cut to CU of ROSA *as Lauren Bacall sitting opposite* ENGLISH. *She smiles. CU of* ENGLISH. *He winks back at her, then starts doing a sketch of her in his notepad.* JEAN HARLOW *brings over the order. Eggs over easy, wholewheat, jelly and coffee. Lots of it. Wide shot of the interior of the diner. Fade.*

Scene 2. Hollywood Boulevard. Evening.

ENGLISH *and* ROSA *(she has slipped out of Lauren Bacall) walk down the Boulevard. Traffic roars and the lights are harsh.*

NARRATOR The neon comes on at 6 p.m. The two lovers stroll down the Boulevard to watch the parade of stars and should-have-beens. A strip of stars stretches the Boulevard but their fantasy movie never got started. For English and his woman, every day is a harsh documentary.

CU of ROSA *looking in the window of Frederick's of Hollywood at a sexy negligé. A pimple festers on her lip.* ENGLISH *looks down and smiles at a star on the pavement. His teeth are stained, he hasn't shaved for days. Pan down his body. A dried piece of yesterday's puke on his left lapel. His jeans sag, his toenails peek through his open sandals.* ROSA *walks ahead and he tries to follow, but he dropped a tab in the diner, and the acid is letting him down. He's scratching, paranoid, panicking.* ROSA *lights a cigarette and places it in his mouth to calm him. They stagger a block or two further, to rest awhile on the pavement outside Grauman's Chinese Theatre. The rest turns to sleep. Cut to wide shot of* ENGLISH *and* ROSA *outside the theatre. Fade to black.*

Scene 3. Hollywood Boulevard. Evening.

Night falls. ENGLISH *is lying on one of the stars on the Boulevard, his notepad still in his hand. Sound of gunfire, a rapid series of shots. Dramatic music. The street sign on the corner of Yucca and Grace. CU of an old woman's face as she is lit by the headlights of a car. She screams. A car screeches to a halt. A dog barks. A figure slips through the shadows into a dark alleyway. Various shots of passers-by. Weird angles. Shocked expressions. Music hits a loud, dissonant chord as we pan down to a man lying on the street. CU of* ROSA *as she turns into shot.*

ROSA Come on, man. If it's a murder, they'll need witnesses, but if it's a movie, they'll need extras. Isn't that the way they found Ginger Rogers?

ENGLISH *looks far gone but manages to stumble along after* ROSA. *She sticks out her tits and rubs the remnants of a lipstick across her mouth. Somehow she pulls it all together, and looks almost stunning in the half-light. Even the zit looks like jewellery. Cut to a group of onlookers around the body.* ROSA *runs into shot. The lighting is perfect for Lauren Bacall. She screams theatrically as she sees the victim, looks around for the camera, and waits for an unseen director to say 'Cut'. A police car has already arrived, and* ROSA, *as Lauren, poses in the headlights, waiting for the close-up. Cut to* LEE MARVIN, *who gets out of the cop car and motions to the onlookers to back off.*

LEE MARVIN There's nothing here for you, folks. Now be good citizens and get on back to your homes.

An ambulance arrives to mop up the carnage. ROSA *and* ENGLISH *are the only ones still there waiting, waiting for the director, the paycheck.* ENGLISH *tries to write something in his notepad, but falls into a heap of garbage cans and is attacked by a dog.* ROSA *beats the dog away with her handbag and drags* ENGLISH *down the Boulevard. She's lost a stiletto, and is limping. Track with them. They are lit by neon and the lights from shop-windows.*

ROSA D'you think it was a night shoot for that new gangster flick?

ENGLISH The set-up was all wrong. It had to be real life.

ROSA No cop says 'Be good citizens' and 'Get on back to your homes', not even in B pictures.

ENGLISH Sometimes they dub the lines on afterwards.

ROSA Maybe the cop actor had to improvise and could only think of a line from some crummy Hopalong Cassidy flick he saw when he was a kid.

Hold shot as ENGLISH *and* ROSA *walk into the distance, towards a cheap neon sign jutting out of a hole in the wall, advertising the Power Pump Bar.* ROSA *and* ENGLISH *enter the bar through a narrow door.*

Scene 4. Interior. Power Pump Bar. Night.

Track along the bar. ENGLISH *and* ROSA *sit next to a little old guy in a golf hat. The old guy is missing most of his teeth, but resembles Mickey Rooney. He rants drunkenly to* ROSA *about how the neighbourhood has gone down. He keeps trying to see down her dress.*

OLD GUY ... and the Brown Derby will never be the same. It's TV that did it, killed off the industry. No matter what they say, it'll never come back. Hey, babe, don't I recognize you from somewhere?

ROSA Not me, mister.

ENGLISH *To Have and Have Not.*

ROSA On a good day I'll pass. Nah, I'm just waiting for a break like everybody else in this town.

OLD GUY I never forget a face. I swear I've seen you somewhere. You're in the business, right?

ROSA *and* ENGLISH *try to talk privately but the* OLD GUY *interrupts.*

OLD GUY I used to be in the industry myself. Song and dance, then stunt work. You name it. Right now I'm in construction. I'm digging up Judy Garland's star outside the Pix movie house and moving it down the Boulevard. That's what I do. Someone else is gonna get walked on for a while.

The OLD GUY *takes a swig of beer and continues to eyeball* ROSA. *Realizing it's a come-on, she bats her eyelids. He smiles, stares at himself in the mirror behind the bar, looks hurt, maudlin.*

OLD GUY One day they're gonna dig up your dreams and turn them into rubble just like mine. It's only there for a while, that fame thing. One day, they're gonna dig up all the stars. The Boulevard will lose its teeth, Sodom and Gomorrah are gonna crumble, the rats are gonna riot in Beverly Hills, and all those fat cats'll be barricaded inside, but the vermin will own the street, and they'll crawl all over the stars on the Boulevard.

OLD GUY *looks over at* ROSA. *Then to* ENGLISH.

OLD GUY You in love with this gal, fella?

ENGLISH *doesn't hear. He carries on doodling. The* OLD GUY *puts down his drink and delivers the rest of his chat-up to* ROSA. *We hear him but the focus is on* ENGLISH. *Track around him with* OLD GUY *and* ROSA *in the background.*

OLD GUY Is he in love with you or in love with a fantasy? Well, if it's unreal, you're in the right place. I swear I've seen your pretty face before.

Various dissolves of ROSA *looking strung out, but trying to look sexy. The barman is watching a ballgame on TV. The* OLD GUY *swigs down his drink and thumps the bar.* ENGLISH *is writing in his notepad. The* BARMAN *brings over a whiskey and puts it down on the counter in front of the* OLD GUY.

OLD GUY Hey, bring my friends the same again.

The OLD GUY *pulls out a clipping from 'Variety' and hands it to* ROSA. *We are behind them, and can see the detail of the clipping as he shows it to her.*

OLD GUY A review I got in 62 for a job I did at Warner's. Thought I was on a roll, but what do you know? I didn't work for ten years. You gotta do what they say. If they offer you a turd on the end of an ice-cream cone you just lick it and say it tastes good. If ever you get hot, remember! Some son of a bitch always wants a piece of you, someone always wants to take your place. The glitter and the sleaze go hand in hand and they call it Hollywood. Swear I've seen you before, babe.

Wide shot of the bar. The OLD GUY *is looking at his reflection.* ROSA *is asleep on his shoulder.* ENGLISH *is maniacally writing. Fade to black.*

Scene 5. Exterior. Hollywood Vista Apartments. Morning.

Crane down a broken-down apartment building. DIRTY DANIEL *sits by the pool. He looks like George Sanders. He's with a young blonde starlet, dancing to cheesy bossa nova muzak. She looks like Marilyn Monroe.*

Cut to angle on entrance lobby. Close up: a pot of freshly brewed coffee simmering. Pan on an ageing resident walking through the corridors, scratching his backside. He opens a door and disappears into his apartment. We follow a Mexican chambermaid pushing a linen trolley. The wheels squeak. The sound continues until we are at ROSA's *door, then cut to* ROSA's *apartment.* ENGLISH *is sitting bolt upright in bed. The curtains are drawn.* ROSA *is sleeping late.* ENGLISH *reaches over and swallows a few pills from the container by the bed. He puts on his pants and stumbles out of the room. The TV is still on from the night before.*

NARRATOR TV is just another drug they can't live without. Reruns of the *Cisco Kid* – and Cal Worthington ads for Dodge cars. The phone is off the hook; the calls come only in fantasy. Everyone wants to be in showbiz.

Exterior of the pool. It's filthy, it hasn't been cleaned for weeks. ENGLISH *swigs down his third coffee and goes over to* DIRTY DANIEL. MARILYN MONROE *is now sobbing hard.* DIRTY DANIEL *thinks he is high class. Spotlessly clean, open-neck shirt, cravat, silk dressing gown, designer shoes. He opens his mouth and his Hispanic accent slips out.*

DIRTY DANIEL English, baby. So good to see you. Couldn't interest you in an acting role? Our leading man just got appendicitis. One hundred cash. This girl. She's great. She does Greek.

ENGLISH *walks straight past, out of shot. We hold on* DANIEL *as he consoles* MARILYN. *Then he gets an idea and we follow him as he walks after* ENGLISH.

DANIEL Hey, what about Rosa? That girl is a star and this chick is versatile. Swings both ways.

MARILYN *looks flattered and smiles coyly at* ENGLISH. *Cut to CU of* ENGLISH. *He looks angry.*

ENGLISH Hey, Daniel. Stay away from Rosa. She's getting into straight acting now.

DANIEL Too bad. She was terrific in *Stud Farm*. I'd use that piece of ass any time.

ENGLISH Maybe. But she's not a piece of ass. She had a walk-on scene in a Lee Marvin flick last night. She even got a close-up.

DANIEL So. I gave her a close-up. She even had the climax.

ENGLISH Yeah, but she's gone legit now. She's going places, Daniel, so fuck off.

DANIEL *gently puts his arm around* MARILYN *and bows towards* ENGLISH.

DANIEL Thank you for the advice. (*To* MARILYN) You see this guy, baby? He thinks he's a hell of a stud. Well, I used him in a scene with his girlfriend once, and he couldn't get it together at the right time. I ended up cutting away to someone else for the money shot. And there he is telling me to fuck off.

ENGLISH (*his hillbilly drawl obvious*) Well, I've told you for the last time, buddy. Stay out of my face.

DANIEL Your loss, buddy, your loss. But remember. Dirty Daniel's always here.

DANIEL *smiles at* ENGLISH *and walks away with* MARILYN. *Wide shot of* ENGLISH *sitting by the pool. He looks tormented. Fade to black.*

Scene 6. Interior. Rosa's Apartment.

Close-up of ENGLISH. *The TV's still on.* ROSA's *clothes are strewn around the room. Her shoes, stockings, dress, lead to the bedroom. He stares at the flickering image on the screen. He looks dejected. Cut to TV screen.* ENGLISH's POV. *A jazz theme plays. We see* ENGLISH *in his own flashback on the screen. The scenes are stylized.*
Flashback sequence:
ENGLISH, *affluent, sitting at a table in the Rat Trap Club. Everyone seems to know him. A pretty topless waitress puts a drink in front of him, but his eyes follow* ROSA's *body as she dances to the saxophone. Cut to* ENGLISH, *checking through 'Variety'. Calendar pages flicker and turn. Cut to* ENGLISH, *down and out, checking through 'Variety'.* ENGLISH *asking* ROSA *for money at the Rat Trap Club. The image on the TV screen returns. You think you're back in real time. But* ROSA *is on the screen. It's a porn movie. She stands out from the other groaning submissives – to* ENGLISH. *She looks into the camera. She looks like she enjoys it.* ENGLISH *joins her on screen. Pan back to reveal a set, to behind the movie camera, and* DIRTY DANIEL *is there.* ROSA *is laughing.* ENGLISH *can't come on cue. Cut to* ENGLISH *picking up* ROSA *from the Rat Trap Club. They walk along Hollywood Boulevard hand in hand. The stars are out. The TV snaps off.*

ENGLISH (*sadly, to himself*) I guess Dirty Daniel *is* always there.

ENGLISH *swallows down a handful of uppers and staggers out on to the Boulevard. He blinks in the sunlight.*

Scene 7. Hollywood Boulevard. Midday.

ENGLISH *shuffles along. Unwashed and unkempt. He sees* HARPO *the violin player dressed in his evening suit, on the ground outside a coffee shop eating a hamburger.*

NARRATOR Seventy-eight degrees. April sunshine. Harpo is a loser. Rosa's body gets bruised by the stares of the Rat Trap Club. The Boulevard is harsh and unsentimental, realistic. That's the way it is.

HARPO Hey, English! I'm going down to the beach. They're shooting a surf movie and they're looking for characters. They'll hire anybody if they look a little crazy. If you look nuts enough, you'll get hired.

ENGLISH Not interested. Why do it? Stand around all day feeling like an idiot for a few dollars.

HARPO Once you would have jumped at the chance. Been first in the queue. Now, you look beaten. Snap out of it. Stay in their face.

Cut to CHARLIE CHAPLIN *outside Grauman's.* HARPO's *POV.*

HARPO Look at Chaplin over there. Once there would have been thousands queueing to see one of his movies. Now, only a few passers-by even acknowledge him. He's too insecure even to leave his pitch. That's the biz. You have to take the ups and downs. I accept it. But you! Now Chaplin, that guy's depressed. Look at those lines on his face. Look at him, then take a look at yourself.

Cut to ENGLISH *scribbling in his notepad.*

HARPO Still writing your movie. Well, good luck with it.

HARPO *hands* ENGLISH *a rolled-up copy of the 'Hollywood Reporter'.*

HARPO Here. Take it. There might be something in it for you. I'm off to the beach. By the way, there's a bash at the Hyatt tonight for a British rock band. Eddie the bellhop said he'd get you in. Who knows, you might meet some real English people. If I don't catch you at the party or the beach, I'll see you on the Boulevard sometime.

ENGLISH's *POV*: HARPO *walks down Hollywood Boulevard dressed in his top hat and tails, holding his violin. He disappears into a crowd. Jazz music plays. A bass line. Then a drum. Builds to a sexy jazz theme.* ENGLISH *puts on his rose-tinted glasses. His POV of the Boulevard as it turns pink.* ENGLISH *snaps his fingers. Straightens up. Gets hip. Starts walking along with confidence. In the distance is Hyatt House. A limousine drives up and stops at the traffic lights.* ENGLISH *looks at the limo and waves. Angle on the limo. Black-tinted windows. Pan off limo as it heads towards the Hyatt, on to* ENGLISH *as he walks into a doorway.*

Scene 8. Interior. Aida Fine Agency.

ENGLISH *walks up behind the pretty girl receptionist and covers her eyes with his hands. He speaks in an English accent. The receptionist smiles. She plays the game for a while.*

ENGLISH Guess who.

RECEPTIONIST Robert Plant. Er. Michael Caine.

ENGLISH *leans down and kisses the receptionist on the lips. She opens her eyes. Looks angry.*

RECEPTIONIST English. You creep.

ENGLISH Tell Miss Fine I am here to see her.

RECEPTIONIST No chance. You can't just walk in to see Aida Fine.

ENGLISH When she sees what I've got she'll crawl on her hands and knees to represent me.

Pan off ENGLISH *up to* AIDA FINE's *office door. He walks into shot just as a fat woman walks out.*

ENGLISH Aida. It's me. English.

AIDA Congratulations. Now get out of my office.

ENGLISH *holds up his crumpled piece of paper.*

ENGLISH But this is a dynamite idea.

AIDA I don't care if it's a cream-cheese bagel. Get your ass outa here. (*Shouts to receptionist*) Hey, honey, will you get me Warner's? I need to speak to Zak Zippel.

ENGLISH (*pretending to know*) Oh yeah. Zak. This is right up his alley. Kinda King Kong meets Godzilla.

AIDA Haven't you heard? Monster flicks are out. Now get lost, you little jerk. I need to go to the bathroom.

We hold shot on AIDA *as she heads towards the bathroom.* ENGLISH *follows her. From his POV we pan up and down* AIDA *as she walks.*

ENGLISH (*voice off*) Miss Fine. I swear I have dynamite right here in my pocket. It's personal, and I didn't really want anyone ever to see it . . .

Camera moves round to AIDA FINE*'s face.*

AIDA OK, jerk. Shoot while I take a crap.

Hold on bathroom door as AIDA *enters.* ENGLISH *hesitates for a moment and then enters the bathroom. We follow as the door swings closed.* AIDA *quickly disappears inside the toilet and closes the door in his face.*

AIDA (*from behind the door*) OK, English. This is your last chance. If I like it, I'll option it and give you your cab fare home. If I hate it, I'll call the police and have you arrested for harassing me in the ladies' bathroom.

ENGLISH *walks over to the mirror and looks at himself. He clenches his fist and goes for it.*

ENGLISH It's a love story loosely based on me and my girl. She came to Hollywood from Mississippi to become a star and for a while it went well. Then she met this guy and they fell in love. Or at least they thought they were in love. Anyway, it ends up that the girl and the guy are unlucky for one another and, instead, the girl's career goes on the skids. The guy can't get any work, and she takes a job as a porn actress to support them both.

We hear the sound of the toilet flushing, then AIDA *walks out.*

AIDA Keep going, babe.

ENGLISH *smiles. Thinks he's on to something.*

ENGLISH The guy gets desperate.

AIDA Robs a bank? What! It's a heist movie. Is that it?

AIDA *takes out some lipstick and starts making up.*

ENGLISH No. He writes a song. He sees all the stars on Hollywood Boulevard and imagines that all the people he sees on the streets are stars who somehow haven't had the lucky breaks. Eventually, the girl gets in with a big-shot producer and leaves the guy. She becomes a big star. He hits the skids and ends up in an asylum. He gets electric shock therapy.

AIDA I like it. You know, Nicholson's looking to direct something right now. This could be the vehicle.

AIDA *readjusts her skirt.*

ENGLISH Then, he gets out of hospital, but he's a vegetable. A vagrant.

AIDA Then, self-redemption. Then, a higher consciousness. Right? Straighten my skirt at the back, will you, babe?

ENGLISH *helps* AIDA *with her skirt.*

ENGLISH He's almost a zombie. Has complete memory loss. The only thing he can remember is the lyrics to the song he wrote while he was with the girl.

AIDA *walks out of the bathroom.* ENGLISH *follows. Camera angle is over* ENGLISH*'s shoulder.*

RECEPTIONIST Zak Zippel on line one, Miss Fine.

AIDA *stops by a water machine and fills a paper cup with water.*

ENGLISH Then he sings on the street, begging for money, and a recording exec drives by in a limo and stops to listen.

AIDA *swigs down the water and gives* ENGLISH *a suspicious look, as if she's heard it all before.*

ENGLISH The guy gets a deal, makes a record of the song and it becomes a hit.

AIDA *exits frame leaving* ENGLISH *in mid sentence.*

ENGLISH The girl's new movie features the song and it wins an Oscar. The guy and the girl meet at the award ceremony and get back together.

ENGLISH *sees that* AIDA *has gone and he chases her into her office. She's on the phone.*

AIDA Zak, I know this movie will get the green light . . .

ENGLISH *looks around the office. Signed photographs of movie stars.* AIDA FINE *with various celebs.*

AIDA . . . Well, let's do lunch and talk about it . . . what? . . . you only want the property if . . . what? . . . we put in a gorilla scene! . . .

ENGLISH *looks at himself in the reflection of a framed Butch Cassidy poster. He lifts up his rose-tinted specs and rubs his eyes. He is beginning to look tired.* AIDA *is still on the phone.*

AIDA OK, Zak. The gorilla is in. We can settle the detail over lunch. Bye, babe.

AIDA *looks up at* ENGLISH.

AIDA You still here?

ENGLISH What about my story?

AIDA To tell you the truth, I liked the story, but I can't represent you. It's too similar to a picture they're developing for Streisand.

ENGLISH *heads for the door.*

AIDA But maybe . . .

AIDA *steps across* ENGLISH *and stands between him and the door.*

AIDA I'll pitch it to Zippel over lunch. Maybe get you a development deal . . . if . . .

ENGLISH If?

AIDA Leave that whore. It's like your story. You're unlucky for one another. I'll help you if you let me, but you've got to play the game my way.

ENGLISH Wow – the casting-couch routine. That's so corny.

AIDA Yeah, but do you know what, handsome? It still works in this town. You gotta know the score by now, babe.

ENGLISH I'll take a raincheck maybe.

AIDA OK, but don't think about it too long. You used to have some pizzazz, but you're looking worse each time I see you. Meanwhile, you know what you should do?

ENGLISH What's that?

AIDA Get a hot band to record the song. That way I can put a package together. Your other alternative is to get out of this town. You're a dreamer, English, but to exist in this place, you've got to get your dreams organized. Otherwise, take a job as a bellhop.

ENGLISH Thanks for the tip, Aida. I'll bear it in mind.

ENGLISH *starts to leave and gives* AIDA *a kiss on the cheek. She faces the camera. We see this moment means more to her than she is willing to show.*

AIDA Now, get lost, and do yourself a favour. Stop living your life on scraps of paper. Get it typed up.

ENGLISH *has already left the office. He hardly hears the last sentence. Cut to wide angle as* ENGLISH *walks past the Hyatt. Zoom to poster advertising a new album by The English Sound.*

Scene 9. Interior. Rosa's Apartment. Afternoon.

ENGLISH *runs in. He shouts out for* ROSA, *who is staggering through from the bedroom in a G-string.* ENGLISH *paces around the room.*

ENGLISH Hey, babe, there's some kind of party for a rock band on the roof of the Hyatt tonight. I'm gonna pitch my idea to them.

ENGLISH *holds up a crumpled piece of paper.*

ENGLISH This is our passport out of here. Eddie the bellhop can get us passes. C'mon baby, move it.

ROSA I have to work.

ENGLISH No problem. We'll go after your set.

ROSA Cool. What do I wear? My stage clothes?

ENGLISH Shake ass, baby. Put something together, will ya.

ENGLISH *is excited. He runs around, putting on hippie beads and after-shave.* ROSA *is nonplussed.*

ENGLISH Throw on a pair of pants. This is rock and roll. This is Hollywood!

ENGLISH *runs out of the house.* ROSA *sees that, in his excitement, he has left the crumpled note. She grabs it and stuffs it into her bag. Loud chords as rock music plays. Fast whip pan to the Rat Trap Club. CU of* ROSA *on stage. The cheap lights give her face a smooth sensual luminescence. No lines. Track out. She's dancing naked. She looks like she's taking her clothes off. Reverse angle showing the audience. The place is half empty. Some cheesy-looking fat slobs, a suspicious-looking thin dude in shades, picking his nails with a switchblade. The music swells. CU of* ROSA *as a bead of sweat appears on her face. She arches backwards. CU of the thin guy leering.*

Scene 10. Interior. The Penthouse of the Hyatt House, Hollywood. Night.

All the glitterati paparazzi celebrazzi. Drag queens and cowboys, débutantes and diplomats, and record execs.

NARRATOR Tonight, everybody can be somebody if they really want to believe it. This is Hollywood. English is a screenwriter and Rosa Lauren Bacall. Celebrity is all.

CU of ENGLISH *as he gets a fix of adrenaline; his face seems to freshen up. Suddenly everybody at the party looks like a celebrity. Even the extras look like stars.* ENGLISH *shouts out as they start to cruise the room. His accent is back to North Carolina.*

ENGLISH Is that Dyan Cannon? Darn, I saw Tab Hunter for a moment. Lord. This is Hollywood, yahoo.

ROSA *sees a film crew doing interviews and makes a beeline.* DIRTY DANIEL *appears with another starlet.* ENGLISH *sees him heading towards* ROSA *and starts chatting, trying to keep him from her.* DANIEL *pulls out a spliff, offers it to* ENGLISH. *CU of* ROSA*'s face as she walks towards the crowd. A saxophone plays. Every step of the way she looks more confident. More beautiful. She reaches the interview and we see a long-haired 1970s* ROCK STAR. *From the back he looks like* ENGLISH. *CU of* ROSA*'s face. Shock.* ROSA*'s POV, a CU of the* ROCK STAR. *It is the double of* ENGLISH. *The* ROCK STAR *gives a seductive wink. Eyeline match to CU of* ROSA. *Love written all over her face. She looks like Lauren Bacall trying to look like an angel. The zit sparkles. The saxophone swells. Slow motion. The* ROCK STAR *approaches* ROSA *slowly. She's almost hypnotized. He runs his hand through her hair. Music reaches a climax. CU of* ROCK STAR. *CU of* ROSA. *The room goes silent. Extreme CU of the* ROCK STAR*'s lips. A low, whispering voice.*

ROCK STAR My room. 502. In thirty-five minutes.

The music of the room fades back. The ROCK STAR *disappears in a crowd of fans.* ROSA *is still staring ahead. She walks through the crowd to where she left* ENGLISH. *He is still talking to* DIRTY DANIEL. *The starlet is still there, he's still smoking the spliff. Track round the two.* ROSA *whispers in* ENGLISH*'s ear. We see both their faces.* ENGLISH *looks shocked, then resigned.* ROSA *kisses him gently on the cheek, winks at* DIRTY DANIEL *and walks away. We hold on* ENGLISH *as he watches her leave. Then he looks at the spliff. Then up at the starlet with big tits and gives a wry smile. Cut to interior. Hotel corridor. We track along from one end of the long corridor. We hear the sound of the elevator opening and closing.* ROSA *comes into shot. She's half-way down the hall, walking away from camera. Follow her as she walks to 502. The door is open. She pauses. There's a clink of glasses and a murmur of voices.* ROSA*'s POV through the door. A typical hotel room, 1970s. Five or six people talking. Sitting in chairs, on the floor, on the bed. The TV is on, but as background.* ROSA *joins* *a pretty girl with curly blonde hair sitting on the bed. The girl turns around. It's Julie Christie. She sounds like she did in 'Doctor Zhivago'.*

JULIE Hello. My name's Julie. What's yours?

ROSA *looks at the girl as if she is crazy but decides to ride it a little.*

ROSA Oh, I'm Lauren. Lauren Bacall.

JULIE *smiles and gives a little toast with her wine glass.*

JULIE A pleasure to meet you, Lauren.

ROSA *is still a little confused. Nervous as she realizes she is with Julie Christie.*

ROSA Where's Warren Beatty? You are still seeing him, aren't you?

JULIE Oh, yes. But he's at another party tonight. I'm just here to support the British.

ROSA *nods slowly, doubtfully.*

ROSA Right.

Pan over to the doorway. The ROCK STAR *has arrived. CU of the* ROCK STAR *smiling at* ROSA *and* JULIE. *Track round as he closes the door.* ROCK STAR *smiles as the door closes on our faces. Fade to black.*

Scene 11. The Boulevard. Early Morning.

ENGLISH *walks slowly towards Zero's diner. In the background there is a billboard advertising Warren Beatty and Julie Christie in 'Shampoo'.* JULIE*'s hair is the same as in the last scene.* ENGLISH *is hovering outside the diner considering his situation. Cut to exterior of a porn cinema. A poster advertising a double bill. 'The Devil in Miss Jones', and 'Deep Throat'.* ENGLISH *forages in his pocket and finds some change, buys a ticket and enters the cinema.*

Cut to footage of porn stars on screen. Cut to medium CU of ENGLISH *watching. Pan out to show the cinema empty; only a few johns. Slow track in on* ENGLISH *as we hear cries of ecstasy on the screen. To full close-up of* ENGLISH. *There are tears in his eyes.*

NARRATOR He remembered the first time he'd kissed her. She could have been a teacher at Sunday school. It's only the things you imagine in a relationship that last. The smiles between words. The spaces. The innuendoes. The unexplained emotion.

ENGLISH *and* ROSA *walking hand in hand on Hollywood Boulevard. Shot like a dream sequence.* ROSA *looks innocent.* ENGLISH *looks clean cut.*

Cut back to hard-core porn on screen. ENGLISH *gets up and walks out.*

Scene 12. Interior. Zero's Diner

ENGLISH *is seated at his usual table. He looks up to see his face reflected in the glass of an old black-and-white photo on the wall. He stares. Cut to* ENGLISH*'s POV as we track along the wall from his reflection to photos of other Hollywood stars.*

NARRATOR Their faces were behind the glass, his was only reflected on it. They were behind it, in the frame. He couldn't fantasize the world any more. His own movie, and he'd cut himself out of the big scene. Now, he was just a bit-part player in a B feature.

Medium shot of ENGLISH *staring straight ahead.* BELA LUGOSI *(in full vampire regalia) sits opposite and reaches across* ENGLISH *for the sugar bowl. One of his vampire teeth falls out. A sad saxophone phrase.* BELA *picks up the tooth and sticks it in his pocket.*

BELA Where's that pretty girl of yours today?

ENGLISH *is jolted. He is in a daze, not quite there.*

ENGLISH Oh, you mean Rosa. She's in Hollywood, pursuing her dreams. I reckon she could be auditioning right this minute.

ENGLISH *slides out from the table as he speaks and walks out of the diner, disorientated. He walks past* BETTE DAVIS, JEAN HARLOW, ZERO MOSTEL. *The usual wannabes. We track with* ENGLISH*'s disorientated point of view down the Boulevard. 'Celluloid Heroes' plays. We see the characters from the song and share* ENGLISH*'s confusion.*

> Don't tread on Greta Garbo as you walk down the boulevard,
> She looks so weak and fragile, that's why she tried to be so hard,
> But they turned her into a princess and they sat her on a throne,
> But she turned her back on stardom because she wanted to be alone.
>
> Rudolph Valentino looks very much alive,
> And he looks up ladies' dresses as they pass sadly by,
> Avoid stepping on Bela Lugosi because he's liable to turn and
>   bite,
> But stand close by Bette Davis because hers was such a lonely life.
>
> If you covered him with garbage, George Sanders would still have
>   style,
> If you stamped on Mickey Rooney, he would still turn around
>   and smile,
> Please don't tread on dearest Marilyn, 'cos she's not very tough,
> She should have been made of iron or steel, but she was only
>   made of flesh and blood.

Music fades under NARRATOR*'s voice.*

NARRATOR Life is not a movie. In the end the credits roll and it's time to confront the real world. ENGLISH had left the frame, but he had to get back. His script needed a rewrite.

Scene 13. Interior. Rosa's Apartment. Night.

TV screen. Old black-and-white melodrama. The goodbye scene. ROSA *is sitting on the bed eating a Hershey bar, watching TV.* ENGLISH*'s crumpled note is on the bed next to her. She has smeared white ointment where the zit was.* ENGLISH *staggers in. There is an uncomfortable silence. The two lovers in the black-and-white movie take over . . .*

MALE LOVER So you have found somebody else.

FEMALE LOVER Oh, yes. Yes. Why try to deny it any longer?

MALE LOVER But why?

FEMALE LOVER He treats me like a woman. He has charm, charisma, wealth. He's everything I want.

ENGLISH *pulls the plug out of the socket. His voice is pure hillbilly, his tone slow and threatening.*

ENGLISH You fucked the rock star, didn't you? Behind my back.

ROSA *thinks for a second, then realizes there's no point in lying.*

ROSA While you were smoking a joint. While you were looking at that chick's tits. While she was probably sucking your dick.

CU of ENGLISH. *He shakes his head in denial.*

ENGLISH I was only talking to her because she was with Dirty Daniel. He had his creepy eyes all over you and I wanted to keep you away. Did you fuck him?

ROSA *falls back on to the bed.*

ROSA I didn't want to tell you. I wanted to spare you. But no, you won't let it go.

ENGLISH But you did screw the guy, right?

ROSA Sure I did. But only after he watched me make out with his road crew.

CU of ENGLISH. *He's in shock. Cut to* ROSA. *She sees his panic and decides to ride it. She moves in close to* ENGLISH's *face.*

ROSA You know why I did it?

ENGLISH *looks as though he is going to throw up. He buries his head in his hands.* ROSA *tries to justify herself.*

ROSA Hey, I was high. I'd taken some uppers at work and one thing led to another. Anyway, I wanted to get the guy to read your story. But you don't wanna hear this.

ENGLISH *looks up. He doesn't seem to care any more.*

ENGLISH But I do. I have to know. Just so that I don't have to imagine it.

There is a tense silence for a moment, but ROSA, *realizing that* ENGLISH *really wants to hear, lights up a cigarette. In the shadowy light, she looks like Lauren Bacall again. Her voice trembles slightly. Slow track around her while she speaks.*

ROSA A roadie. An English dude. Took me from behind. Then afterwards got me to kneel down on the floor while he lay on his back and licked me. While this was happening, I gave the rest of the crew some head. Is that what you want me to say happened?

ENGLISH *is now in shot. He is beyond despair, verging on the comical.*

ENGLISH It must have really been romantic. Did they give you a back-stage pass?

ROSA *looks angry and stubs out her cigarette.*

ROSA Look, you got some kind of evil mind, mister. What do you take me for? Hell, I would only do that kind of thing to pay the rent and you know it.

ENGLISH But the rock star? You did . . . didn't you?

ROSA *gets up from the bed and runs over to* ENGLISH *in a dramatic gesture. She cups his face in her hands, but he pulls away. He starts putting a few things in a bag.* ROSA *follows him. CU of* ROSA, *her face lit as in the porn movie. Tense music.*

ROSA OK, so I went with the rock star. And, boy, do I feel shitty about it now. I kept thinking about you. He was like all the things you said you wanted to be and had been all the places you want to go. I always thought they were the reasons I stayed with you, but do you know something? It made me realize that I prefer the dream to the real thing. No rock star can take me away from you. Sure, I was screwed by him, but we all get screwed one way or another. I shake my bare ass everyday so we can stay here together. So I can be with you.

ENGLISH *walks into the kitchen. He looks up at his reflection in the window. Melodramatic chords.*

ENGLISH But you did it. And you stayed.

ROSA *walks into shot behind him. The music changes mood. A sweet violin plays a sad melody.*

ROSA I fell asleep. When I woke up I reached over for you and it was him. He said that I was saying your name in my sleep and that I must really be in love with you.

ENGLISH He said that?

ROSA Then he got me to tell him all about you, and how you wanna write scripts and direct movies an' all. He says he wants me to go to London with him but I said I would only go if you came along. You know what he said? He said, sure.

There is an awkward silence. They are standing by the kitchen sink and ENGLISH *is turning the tap on and off.*

ROSA Then he started talking about how some people imagine they're in the movies all their lives and never get to be on a movie screen. But he said that was good, because then, they'll never age. Never have to watch their careers fade. Then he said something weird, like he was afraid to see his looks go, to get old. He cried a bit. I had to get out of there. If that's stardom, you can keep it. I prefer the movie you imagine me to be in. It's called life.

Music swells up in the background.

ROSA By the way, your film idea. It's really sad. Is that the way we are? Bad for one another?

ENGLISH Nah, it's just a fantasy. You're good for me, baby.

ENGLISH *looks* ROSA *in the eyes and then sees the white ointment on her mouth. He smiles.*

ENGLISH I preferred you with the zit.

ENGLISH *and* ROSA *embrace by the kitchen sink.*

Scene 14. Hollywood Boulevard. Night.

We follow ENGLISH *and* ROSA *as they walk along hand in hand, tip-toeing around the stars. They are somewhere in between reality and fantasy. We hear* ROSA, *off camera.*

ROSA Hey, guess who else I met? Julie Christie. God. She was so kind. But the silliest thing happened. Some idiot came in to clear the room and threw her out because they thought she was a groupie. And the joke was they let me stay. Boy, did I feel like a celebrity or what?

ENGLISH That wasn't Julie Christie.

ROSA Sure was.

ENGLISH Nah. She wasn't a movie star. She was just another dreamer. Like me and you.

We hold on a shot of the Boulevard as ROSA *and* ENGLISH *embrace before walking into the distance. Cut to the entrance of the Pix movie house.* HARPO MARX *stands playing his violin. We pan down the stars on the street. Slow fade to black. Music builds. Credits.*

■

Everybody's a dreamer and everybody's a star,
And everybody's in movies, it doesn't matter who you are,
There are stars in every city, in every house and on every street,
And if you walk down Hollywood Boulevard their names are
    written in concrete.

You can see all the stars as you walk down Hollywood Boulevard,
Some that you recognize, some that you've hardly even heard of,
People who worked, suffered, struggled for fame,
Some who succeeded, some who suffered in vain.

Everybody's a dreamer, and everybody's a star,
And everybody's in showbiz, it doesn't matter who you are,
But those who are successful, be always on your guard,
Success walks hand in hand with failure on the Hollywood
    Boulevard.

I wish my life was a non-stop Hollywood movie show,
A fantasy world of celluloid villains and heroes,
Because celluloid heroes never feel any pain,
And celluloid heroes never really die.

Voices in the Dark

Muriel was, according to the experts who determine this sort of thing, mentally ill. When the doctor made it official, it had come as a relief. All the years of family whispers, innuendo, gossip and rumour. The silence that descended whenever she walked into a room. The concerned, condescending relatives who offered her cups of tea and asked after her could now classify their unease: Muriel was 'mentally ill'.

Muriel sat on the bench, next to the pond in Regent's Park. She felt as always. The world was still a strange, uncompromising place where weakness was a sin and inward-looking individuals were irresponsible and not to be trusted. She would still wake every night to the sound of her own voice shouting out that she was afraid. Each step she took was still uncertain. Silence was her means of survival. She was withdrawn, and she blamed her family for making her so. Communication was difficult. She would not give herself away, and in case anyone got close, her silence would shut them out.

The doctors thought it might be hereditary. They'd asked if there was madness in the family. Her father had been a mild alcoholic, but there was no way he could have been described as mad. It was her father's normality that was striking. His only weakness was tears – he would become almost too emotional at times. In an age when men were not supposed to cry, Muriel's father would weep. A sad movie or a sentimental song lyric would break him up. It caused her mother some embarrassment. At the Christmas pantomime, it was not Muriel who had a lump in her throat when the wicked sisters made Cinderella stay at home, but Muriel's sensitive father. It was Mother who was the strong one. When Muriel's husband left her for a younger woman, Mother screamed out that she would have him castrated. Her father had wept on the doorstep. When the divorce was final, Muriel went into total withdrawal.

There were no children. She had never been the prettiest, and had found it difficult as a teenager to talk to the men who chatted her up at the Saturday-night dance. Her relationship over, her self-confidence went. She became frightened and withdrew. Too afraid to reveal the smallest emotion.

When her father died of a stroke she felt sorrow but could cry no tears. She drank to exorcise the pent-up feelings. She released her emotions and was prescribed Valium to keep her down, and anti-depressants to keep her from going too far. When drinking she showed signs of paranoia. She thought she was being followed. According to Muriel, her ex-husband had hired the milkman to spy on her, to reduce his alimony payments. More medication. Eventually Muriel's parents were persuaded to put her in an institution. She was unable to cope with her own emotions.

'Take the pills. We want you to take the pills.'

The doctor's voice was very exacting. Muriel had been brought up to believe that when a doctor told you to take pills, you took them. There was no argument. Doctor knows best. But still there was a nagging feeling inside; the pills only camouflaged her real feelings. She wanted to confront how she felt, face the consequences. Inside she felt strong and confident, but as soon as she tried to speak, her words stuttered out, almost incoherently.

'Just a few days. See what it feels like. No pills.'

The senior doctor closed his file. He was losing his patience. The junior doctor was more compassionate.

'A few days is not enough, you will need these pills for a long time. We'll tell you when to stop.'

Muriel felt a surge of desperation in the pit of her stomach. The medication made her feel this way. Her chemical balance had been turned around. Was her real self so terrifying it *had* to be tamed with medication? Should she be afraid to confront it? Was that what they were telling her? The arguments knotted her inside and she went with her gut feeling.

'But I want to feel things. I want to feel anger, sadness. I don't want it blacked out. I want . . . I want to be myself, whatever that is. However bad it makes me feel.'

The senior doctor looked at his watch. A nurse came and took Muriel back to her ward. On the way she passed an elderly woman patient shuffling along the hallway, eyes down.

Muriel must have looked that way for a time. She remembered arriving here. They took down her particulars, gave her pills to swallow. Certain times of day, certain colour pills, certain quantities. After a few days it became a ritual. She couldn't recall when the stooping and the shuffling began. And always that taste in the back of her mouth. Like chemical emotion. Dry mouth and hair. Dandruff. Her lips cracked even when she covered them in Vaseline. Her hands were sore. There seemed no point in eating. She did sit-ups at first, but the will to keep her body active only lasted a few days. It only stimulated more thought as the blood pumped ideas and fears through her brain. The sleeping pills no longer worked. Eventually she would drift off, but not before the late-night chorus of wails and cries from the other patients.

For the first week she couldn't look at herself in the mirror. She was terrified of what she might see. Then one day she caught her reflection in the window of the recreation room. She looked haggard, much older. She had abandoned the ritual of make-up, and her hair was tied back carelessly in a bun. Strands of long, grey hair showed through the faded auburn rinse. She looked around at some of the other patients and saw that they all looked the same. She laughed out loud. That's what mad people do, isn't it? Laugh out loud.

The inmates were an assortment of society's rejects. She did find one ally in Trevor, a twenty-four-year-old office clerk. He heard voices telling him to murder his parents, and he was being tested for schizophrenia. Muriel saw his parents one visiting day. The mother was a pamperer and the father an ex-army type, he only spoke at his son. Maybe the voices were talking sense. Trevor was a friendly young chap, a very good chess player and a willing listener to anyone's problems. He'd support Muriel during the day, and it was only at night that he showed any sign of illness. His eyes would glaze over as if he was drifting off into another world, he had to submit to his own demons. She felt for him, but she couldn't cry. Not even when he broke down completely. He was taken away and she never saw him again. She missed him, but the medication seemed to block her tears. It blocked up the original hurt but it also blocked her reactions and feelings, compassion, sadness, elation. Surely this wasn't normal? Was this the normal range of emotions? Muriel listened anxiously as the doctor read her report.

'They say that you must stay on the medication. Are you happy with that?'

Muriel was silent. If she said nothing the doctor would make up his own mind. She was too terrified of making a comment, the fear of being judged. The staff took notes when she spoke in the hospital, as if they were compiling a dossier against her. The doctor continued his questioning.

'It says here that you are afraid of everything. Distrustful of everyone. You dislike the medication being prescribed to you.'

The doctor sneered.

'You must snap out of this, madam, or face the consequences. Paranoid neurosis.'

It sounded to Muriel as if he was talking about someone else. Muriel had been feeling more and more detached from herself.

'You are afraid of being in confined spaces. Cannot sleep. Difficulty communicating.'

The doctor's list of symptoms made Muriel cringe. Surely there was no way she would be let into the outside world. At least inside she was safe, for the time being. She wasn't well enough to become an out-patient. The doctor thought she was. When the truth impacted on her, she panicked. But no matter how she protested, the doctor emitted a stubborn charm. He knew best.

She stayed with her family for a while, but communication was even more difficult. She had run away, to a bed and breakfast at first, but she had run out of money. She spent the following days wandering around central London. She was only doing this long enough for the pills to run out. The weather was not too bad, so she slept rough. She hated being around the other dossers because she did not feel like one of them. They were the sick and needy ones. There was no way back for them. Muriel would eventually come off the pills and have the strength to confront her feelings and her family. There weren't many pills left now.

She had established her pitch in Regent's Park. Some of the lunch-time regulars would offer her sandwiches, but she wasn't going to fall for that old trick. She wouldn't let anyone feel she owed them something. If people spoke to her, she would stare into space and say nothing. As though she was not in the same world. After a while people forgot she was there and talked in front of her. They revealed their own secrets and fears. Most of the people she encountered needed some sort of emotional support. Muriel had reached the conclusion that the world was a mad-house, but she was sheltered by her silence. Silence was power. The desperate ones came alone to talk to her. With them she felt she was in control. She waited until they'd gone before scrounging through the bins for leftovers. Then she'd tear up the crumbs of bread and sit contentedly with the pigeons. When someone came by she would stare ahead, her eyes glazed. She decided she was a doctor of the human spirit. The word must have spread about this Florence Nightingale on a park bench. And all because she never said a word. Only listened. People in need received her messages telepathically and came to blurt out their inner fears. She connected with a person's psyche and they went away cleansed after pouring out their problems in Muriel's deaf ears. Businessmen told her corporate problems, and lovers tales of violence.

One man, a commuter in a pinstripe suit, said he was a mass murderer. He had attacked women and had become known as the Surrey rapist. A boastful man with small sharp features. Surely he was too boring to be a rapist or a murderer? Muriel dismissed him as a crank fantasizing for some excitement. Now, Trevor could have been a killer. He could play chess, after all. This dim little suburbanite was just some insidious wanker who liked talking dirty to deaf old ladies on his daily commute. Her suspicions were confirmed when the traveller confided that a well-known songwriter was plundering his character for a drama-documentary. He was a complete fantasist. He should be put away. The next time he came she got up and walked away. The man was left mid sentence, boasting of sex in a toilet on a train. He looked crushed, and she took her final pill. The next day, she started feeling sorry for him, imagining him squashed under a train. Her emotions twisted and turned, but there were no tears. In the effort she bit through her bottom lip, and blood spurted on to her cardigan like jam from a fat doughnut. She saw a still-smouldering cigarette on the ground and burned the palm of her hand, but she didn't feel the pain.

A few days later, an artist sat and drew her. His name was Fox and he'd been a criminal all his life. He'd been in Borstal, and then spent so much time in prison that the thought of going outside terrified him. He'd feigned madness, and done such a good job that he was almost given a lobotomy. He was sectioned and given so much medication he lost his identity. He started to believe he was William Blake, studying his religious drawings and memorizing the sacred hymns. He'd got into a fight with another inmate, who interrupted him singing his masterpiece, 'Jerusalem', and battered him around the head. He was sent to a prison for the criminally insane. Written off. It was then that the voices had told him to become a painter. His art would bring him back and make life easier to cope with. Now he was out, and spent his time painting delicate pictures of the squirrels and pigeons in Regent's Park. Sailing boats on the Serpentine, yachts and ocean-liners on the Thames. He painted isolated figures on park benches like Muriel. He still conversed with the angels as they floated above the trees. Said he could see the souls of the dead clapping with joy as they ascended to heaven. In the picture he'd painted of her, a guardian angel looked over her shoulder. Fox said it was a loved one who had departed. Perhaps a friend from a past life. Possibly the soul of someone close about to die. The image reminded her of her mother. Fox said that his own mother would be proud of him, with his creative streak, she always wanted more than juvenile delinquency for her son. Muriel thought about her mother. She remembered feeling home-sick when her mother had first visited her in hospital. Muriel wanted to see her again. Her distrust of the world was overcome by the urge. Perhaps she could stay in her mother's flat long enough to get off the drugs, and feel a genuine emotion again. Anything. A smile. A tear. And no side effects. The following day a young man sat on the bench next to her and told her about the daughter he had lost through divorce. As he ran off down the path, Muriel broke her silence.

'Goodbye.'

The sound of her own voice surprised her. She stared out at the ducks and thought about going home. She felt strong enough now to feel the pain.

WATERLOO SUNSET

Voices in the subway,
Looking for the overground,
Echoes in the darkness,
Lonely cries within a sound.

A voice that has no face,
Is lost in time, an inner space,
Chasing dreams that got lost in the dark,
Reaching out, always searching,
Lonely voices in the dark.

The Deal

Richard Tennant rarely made notes. He considered it bad form to put such intimate details on to paper. Notes could, in certain situations, be used as incriminating evidence; sometimes they were more damning than any eye-witness or forensic proof. They often conveyed a person's state of mind, how they really felt. A barrister friend of Richard's had once based an entire legal argument solely on a scrap of paper, with notes scribbled on it. It showed intent. Typed letters on headed paper were often contrived; in many ways they put forward a point of view. As he flew to New York on Concorde Richard was presented with the usual gift pack of stationery, and a little grey notebook was handed to him by the steward. Normally, Richard would have left it behind but as he flew out to meet Lester Mulligan he felt a sudden urge to document his meetings, to heighten and expand the detail, in case it would serve him further on down the line. Richard's longhand was impressive. His public-school education was inscribed in it, and it had the authority of a doctor's prescription.

29 March

Flew out to see Lester Mulligan via New York. Good prospects for deal here. Have seen his company accounts. The decreasing profits will lead to bankruptcy. Confident of result.

30 March

Flight to LA delayed. Opportunity to see Dr Neuberg for a check-up. Will probably get the same lecture about smoking-drinking-late nights etc., but what the hell.

1 April

Hope the date isn't too significant. Fools' day. Meet Mulligan tonight to talk over the deal. He sounds like a complete casualty on the phone. Try to perk him up a bit. He depresses me. Makes me think of my own shortcomings. Was warned he would be a tricky character. Perhaps this is part of the act.

2 April

Meeting at United Records. Morton Sosa, Annette Fabrizzi, Lester Mulligan and myself. (Get detail typed up and issued as a memorandum.)

Meeting was arranged for 2.30 p.m. but had to be put back because Morton Sosa was delayed. Lester and I shown around the offices by one of Sosa's assistants, and ushered into his office at approximately 3.15 p.m. The great man burst into the room about ten minutes later. I was concerned about lateness of Sosa's arrival. Worried he was not serious about the deal. But Sosa is big-time enough not to string us out unnecessarily. Did his best to apologize in his own way by offering us front-row seats to the LA Lakers. I hate basketball but was obliged to accept. (The things I do for my clients.) Lester sat impassively throughout the meeting, almost as if he was unconnected to it all. Sosa was boiling over with enthusiasm about 'doing business with such a rare talent as Lester Mulligan'. Reassuring, but I could still have done with a cigarette. No qualms normally, but Sosa is on a health kick. Fresh orange juice and gymnasiums.

He cuts a dash. He could've been half South American or Italian, but 'Morton' had to be white Anglo-Saxon Protestant. This wasp had a sting in its tail. He's been on the corporate circuit quite a while. He had been at all the majors at one time or another. An athletic-looking fifty-something. Still had a good physique, pumped-up muscles rippling through his Armani suit. Still turned a few heads. Probably educated at Harvard or Yale. Knew my background and made unnecessary comparisons of English and American education. His hair is slightly thinning on top, but even that seemed to add to his appeal. He seemed to know how to make all his assets work for him. Hopefully, Les would become one of them. The only hint of a fault was a slight lisp – it made him talk out of the side of his mouth whenever he was agitated – and a sliced left ear. He had all the ammunition for survival in the industry – the mannered academic went halves with the cut-throat Latin hood. He turned ugly when he negotiated. He knew all the corporate games, where all the corporate skeletons were buried. He knew the details of every rival's climb, their manipulations, manoeuvres, hustles. He had learned his trade, and on the totem pole of power, no one stood higher than Morton Sosa. He reminded me a little of the great San Francisco promoter Bill Graham, but without Graham's down-to-earth charm. Legend had it that Sosa once fell out with Graham over radio advertising, and even Graham didn't dare fuck with him. Les thought it, I knew it, and Morton Sosa believed it. No one fucked with Morton. You worked with him until he fucked you. Then, you thanked him for the experience and moved on. And when you managed to crawl your way into a position of seniority, you took his calls.

Annette Fabrizzi seemed a sweetheart. Her name conjured up

an exotic Italian flame, but she was cool and serene. She came from a respected Connecticut family who made their fortune out of cardboard packaging and heavy-goods delivery. A good background for business affairs at a record company. She was pushing the deal to Les. She said his work had inspired her. Lester knew he was a few things to different people, but he was flattered to inspire the head of business affairs at United. Morton butted in before I could move to close the deal.

'Assuming the numbers add up.'

Annette had done her research and calmly rattled off the meagre sales of Les's last album. Les smiled weakly. Morton beamed.

'We've gotta do better than that, otherwise we're all out of the business.'

I couldn't help thinking it was a veiled threat – if Lester's album didn't sell, we would be out of the business.

Les left the room and we discussed some figures. I pitched high knowing they would halve it. Sosa said he hoped Les's new songs would be cutting-edge material. Hard rock, but with intelligent lyrics. Then he made a request that left me puzzled. He wanted Les to record 'Waterloo Sunset'. (Hardly new. Or cutting edge.) Had a feeling Sosa didn't even know the tune but had read the title somewhere. I knew Les wanted to record only new material, but thought it best not to mention it. We shook hands and agreed to meet later that week.

3 April

Les called. Launched into a tirade. Said he thought Morton Sosa was a vulgar Colombian scumbag. That no amount of money would make him sign with United. I tried to calm him, and reminded him of his financial position. Then, out of the blue, he asked if I was wearing my Hilditch and Key shirt. I told him I was. I was wearing my Ralph Lauren. Then he talked about Annette. Les liked Annette. A hopeful sign. I must make sure she attends as many of the meetings as possible. Les took the Red-Eye to New York. I'm staying on for a day or two.

Note: Must arrange for half a dozen Hilditch and Key shirts to be delivered before my next meeting with Les.

Call Miami. Get an update.

Ask Dr Neuberg to check me in for tests next time in New York.

4 April, 2.30 a.m.

Les called to ask me to switch on my fax. He sent through some ideas, scribbled down in longhand. The notes are rather vague but I suppose it's a relief to see he hasn't dried up.

3.30 a.m.

Just nodding off when Les called again asking if I liked the fax. Then he mumbled something about it being time to confront the demons. Oh dear.

Scattered

The Thirty-Two-Bar Bridge

It was time for a clear-out. Les looked around the apartment. Everything in it seemed disposable. The occasional tables would no doubt find an owner. The lampshades could go. He'd bought them in a sale at Macy's. They'd looked like white accordions, but the dust had settled inside the cracks and tarnished them. The settee had seen better days. If that settee could talk. The conversations, all the promises made on it, all the laughs, the unplanned stop-overs. The times he had fallen asleep watching television and woken up with that sour taste in his mouth, with the television still on. The Indian rug in the living room was discoloured and the patterns had disappeared. A thick film of dust had formed around the edges of the parquet floor. All this would soon go. Somebody else would come in, clean it up, throw out the garbage and start again. Perhaps they would have better luck. There was only one room he couldn't face. He opened the door and turned on the light in the closet. He looked ahead, a couple of rows of vinyl LPs stacked on a shelf. Old videos, correspondence, books, bottles of beer and wine, discarded clothes hanging shoddily on a small rail. Mementoes picked up over the years from friends and fans. An old walking stick from when he broke his toe. Cardboard boxes full of old newspapers and scribbled diaries, never completed. Sketch books full of blank pages of pictures that were never drawn. An old biscuit tin full of loose change and boxes of matches from restaurants. Where should he start? Should he just close the door behind him and hope that it would shut away all this débris of a lifetime? He could blowtorch the lot. But it wouldn't be fair on the other residents in the high-rise apartment block.

He could see a part of himself in all these remnants. Like his own private museum. Someone would come along and draw conclusions, from the assorted memorabilia, the letters, the documents, the contracts, the insurance policies. In an old shoebox he found more matches and receipts from restaurants, one from a place on Columbus Avenue where he ate the night Wall Street crashed. Black Tuesday, 1987. That had cleaned the restaurants out. Anybody could have got a seat. People were suddenly ordering take-aways. The bubble had burst. A little pocket diary for 1987. Flicking through the pages, the day-to-day entries took him into flashback. The entries had stopped suddenly. He caught sight of a miniature bottle of Guinness, from a souvenir shop. Carol had given it to him.

She was a dancer with wild red flowing hair and large blue eyes. When he had first met her in the artists' bar at the theatre, her hair had been neatly tied in a bun on the top of her head. On stage her face was so expressive, he'd focused on her alone. The picture of artistic elegance, a sleek dancer with bad feet for classical ballet. She would stuff tissues in the front of her point shoes so it looked as if her foot arched perfectly. And always those beautiful eyes that exposed her wild restless soul, penetrating, persuasive and ethereal. She was also a superb drinkist. Pints of Guinness no problem. A brandy or two to follow before the demons came and those eyes took you on a journey of the twilight world, searching for answers to desperate questions. He remembered seeing her lying naked in bed in her little attic flat in Montenotte, overlooking Cork city. Her tough, athletic body carried a lifetime of injuries. Bunions, torn Achilles', pulled muscles, inflamed joints, traumatized ligaments and damaged tendons. All the while she continued to dance. Now the dance was nearly over. There she was, staring up at the ceiling. At nothing. Her career had ended with a half-empty house at the Cork Everyman. The audience clapped hard and long, but Carol vanished back to her dressing room, almost embarrassed to draw attention to herself on her final night. The stage manager gave her a small bouquet, and after the quickest of goodbyes she was out of the back door and walking along, past the bridges, over the river Lee. She ended up at Dan Lowrey's in McCurtain Street, standing at the bar, a pint of stout in her hand. Now, it seemed, she had nothing to stay fit for. But still the visits to the doctor to put the injuries right – for normal employ. Once the dance stops, the injuries come thick and fast, and don't go away. Physiotherapy for the hip. Body maintenance that should have been done long ago, but the dancers' schedule did not permit. Then an opportunity to dance again, an audition for a special production, and only to be told that her point work had never been up to scratch. The devastation of rejection. The damaged pride when word got out she had been rejected, that her chance of a comeback had been stifled.

Walking across the bridge towards the cobbled steps of Patrick's Hill, past the bars on McCurtain Street and up to her flat in Montenotte Hill, she remembered happier times. When she'd come from Waterford to be a founding member of the company. Rehearsals in a damp dance studio. Long tours through Ireland, dancing classical, contemporary and traditional, for intellectuals, farmers, nuns, politicians, 'friends of the ballet'. The company was packed tight in a coach with no suspension and every bumpy road left its mark. The affairs between the dancers. The scandals and gossip about gay lovers. The on-stage farting and loud belches at rehearsals. The foreign divas who came to guest. Members of the corps. They had come from all over – Canada, Monte Carlo, Bucharest and Balti-more – to dance in the ballet. The time when she danced 'The Playboy' in New York. They're memories now, used to build her self-esteem. Build up the courage to face the world, take the job as the waitress to put something in the bank. It was in a bar close to the ballet company. She'd try to show no bitterness when the dancers came in. There she was, the principal dancer, waiting tables and serving drinks to beginners. She complained of a nagging chest cold that never seemed to go away. A visit to the doctor, and days after in hospital with leukaemia. Those eyes darkened by blindness as the disease spreads.

The new ballet opens at the opera house. Word is out it will save the company, and its grant will be reinstated.

A nun sits by Carol's bed in the hospital. Carol tells her that she is not afraid. Her eyes cannot see but they still seem to stare at the heavens. The nun gently closes Carol's eyes. The curtain falls on the ballet. The stage is dark. The company folds.

When writers compose songs, they usually make the middle last only eight bars – the middle eight or bridge. It takes you from one part of the song to another. Sometimes a memory sticks and won't go away. It makes you want to keep the bridge going just that little bit longer.

I look around that empty room,
No sight nor sound, she left so soon,
She's out of view and yet I find those scattered clues she left behind.
A photograph with her smiling face,
A cigarette stubbed out on the fireplace,
A coffee cup with her lipstick stains,
I guess I'll never see her again.

Ever since she went away, I've been alone to contemplate,
Time and space and why worlds move.
While sitting in my solitude,
I've watched the stars and wondered why they're scattered up
    there in the sky.
And is she up there out of view on some higher platitude?
I wish I knew, wish I could prove the reason why this life on earth is
Scattered like the universe.

Holiday Romance

It was the time of grand hotels, seaside resorts, spa towns and palm courts, of coffee mornings and gatherings on the terrace at the Mount Bay Hotel on the south coast of England. The smell of fried breakfasts and the sound of clinking teacups; genteel rustling of the morning papers; cranky old soldiers and retired matrons. Strolls along the windy pier, along the cliff tops, misty clouds covering the esplanade and seagulls mocking the huddled-up hikers returning to safe haven and an afternoon tea of cucumber sandwiches. A nap in the amicable surroundings of the library, then a quick spruce-up in time for a gin and tonic or a dry sherry, as the soft string quartet wafts through the velvet corridors. The dinner gong sounds and the guests respond, to be served by fussy young girls in ill-fitting uniforms with the roast of the day. Afterwards a dance, the quartet playing waltzes and two-steps. It was a time when things seemed to move more slowly. When people engaged in muted chit-chat, when drinks were on account and cheques were accepted without plastic as back-up, when people dressed for dinner. Before surveillance cameras and alarms, before conversation was replaced by wallpaper music. This was a time long ago, when Lavinia was a young woman, in her prime. The time between wars, when the leisured classes drifted through each day with elegant ease, and romance beckoned from every corner. Ladies of fashion were courted by eligible young gentlemen, society scandals were discussed behind flickering eyelashes and acts of courage and chivalry applauded. It was a time of manners and good taste, before the world counted time with a stop-watch. This was the time Lavinia remembered.

The gay world of her youth seemed so far removed from her little mansion flat in W1. Now young people listened to rave music, took drugs and danced alone. Every day she looked out from her window at the tourists on their way to Madame Tussauds. The turbulent traffic on the Marylebone road never seemed to let up. Its relentless growl hovered outside the window. It was all so different from that time. Only her memories and the mantelshelf mementoes took her back. A picture of herself and Geoffrey dressed for the Christmas ball at the Brighton Metropole. 1938. Or was it 39? Lavinia was unsure. The years moved by so quickly. The only year that stood out was 1977, the year that Geoffrey had died. It had started as a cold, shortly after a dinner and dance for the Jubilee. It developed into pneumonia and, within a month, Geoff was dead. So sudden. Almost without fuss. In death as in life, almost apologetic for causing so much aggravation. He'd made sure she would be financially secure. A healthy endowment policy and his army pension meant she would not have to struggle.

Even so, the money could not disguise the fact that Lavinia's existence was empty with Geoff gone. Her trips down the Marylebone road to Oxford Street weren't the same. She could cope, but in no way was Lavinia still a lady of leisure. Inflation had eroded most of her savings, and in many ways she was relieved that Geoff was not around to see her descent into genteel poverty.

Geoffrey had fought in the Second World War so, like many women of her generation, Lavinia had been alone for months on end. Geoff had been based in Middlesex, and they had arranged a weekend on the south coast together, away from the air raids and black-outs of London, but at the last moment he'd had to cancel. Rather than lose the deposit, he suggested that Lavinia spend the weekend at the hotel. It was that weekend in Bournemouth that

Lavinia had met him. 12 August 1942. She remembered the date. She remembered his name . . .

They were the only two people alone in the hotel that evening, and a thoughtful waitress had suggested that they share a table for dinner. Surely it was harmless enough? No one would know, and it would be nice to chat to somebody, rather than sitting listening to other people's conversations.

At the table they asked each other where they lived, where they had grown up, but somehow no reference was made to husbands and wives. No innuendo, no amorous advances, but Lavinia felt some connection between them. He was called Guy and was on a short vacation after a spell in a convalescent home. He was a little vague about it, but it was something to do with an injury sustained during an air raid.

His hair was dark, slicked back and slightly thinning on top, which made him look like Noël Coward. He even had that clipped upper-class accent that was very fashionable at the time. His suit was immaculately pressed, had a dashing cut and looked remarkably new considering the wartime shortages. Maybe he worked in the fashion industry. The more she talked to Guy, the less Lavinia thought about the war – the rationing and the fear of defeat were forgotten. In fact, the more they talked, the less she thought about anything except Guy and how thoroughly entertaining he was. His lips pursed slightly as he spoke, and she couldn't quite pin down the accent. There was a hint of Scottish in the way he ended certain sentences and a kind of drawl to certain words, as if he had seen too many Westerns. His behaviour was impeccable, his wit charming and sophisticated, his manners faultless – but then he ordered claret with the fish, a pint of bitter when the dessert trolley came, and a pickled onion to eat with his cheese. It seemed so uncharacteristic.

After dinner the string quartet struck up. Before the war there would have been an orchestra, but most of the musicians had joined the war effort, leaving only the quartet – an elderly woman and three rather bashful young girls. There was an uncomfortable edge to their playing, which tended to grind on the ear, but made the occasional harmonies all the more satisfying. Then they struck up a quickstep, and Guy asked Lavinia to dance. Surely it would do no harm?

He danced beautifully. Geoffrey was no slouch on the dance-floor, but compared to Guy he was a complete beginner. Guy made Lavinia feel as though she was floating on air, and the closer he held her, the tighter she held on to him, as if she was on a merry-go-round at the fair and Guy was the only thing stopping her from falling. His shortcomings at the dinner table were forgotten as heads turned and eyebrows were raised. They were the centre of attention. Guy grabbed Lavinia by the arm and spun her around, leapt in the air and slid across the dance-floor on his knees in a move that rivalled Jack Buchanan or even Fred Astaire. Lavinia blushed. She was not used to causing so much commotion. Geoffrey was a sombre companion, unlike the exhibitionist she found herself dancing with. Then Guy took over and invited all the hotel guests on to the floor to do the Lambeth Walk. By the end of the night Lavinia was in a complete daze. She admitted secretly that she had never had so much fun. As she stood back and watched Guy organizing the dance, she noticed how delicately he seemed to move.

Everything she noticed in him, she compared with Geoffrey – and her husband came off unfavourably. There had never been anyone other than Geoff, but now, for the first time, came the unsettling thought that, perhaps, she could have met someone different, could have married someone else . . .

Most of the guests had retired to their rooms. Guy seemed nervous. Did he think she wanted him to make a pass at her? Lavinia had no expectations of any romantic interlude. Far from it. In many ways, Guy was acting as he should. It was just that he had seemed so forward and dashing earlier. He was shocked when Lavinia suggested that they join the few remaining guests, who were going skinny-dipping; she had to drag him along. It was so liberating to be with him. As if he had made her come out of her own shell and start to enjoy life. She hadn't forgotten Geoffrey – she was just taking the opportunity to forget the war, to take in some sea air, and live for a few days.

When they got to the beach, the nude bathing was in full flow. Lavinia was taken aback by the sight of the quartet of prim ladies baring all and frolicking in the chilly sea. Earlier, Guy had seemed a lusty sort, in many ways a womanizer, but now, under the moonlight, Lavinia could see a look of reticence bordering on coy disgust. He was almost brooding.

By the time she'd dried off and had a sip of brandy from a Thermos, Guy had disappeared back to his room. The following morning she saw him at breakfast. They even went for a stroll on the beach afterwards, but the night before was not mentioned. Lavinia explained that Geoffrey was coming to join her that day. She felt that she was distancing herself from Guy already, as if her imaginings of a deeper intimacy had been reality. Deep down Lavinia wanted something to feel guilty about, an encounter of her own, a dark secret she could take with her, back to Geoffrey, something to fantasize about whenever life became a little too dull. Guy took her for tea and crumpets and bought her a cheap, cheeky postcard. They didn't speak after their return, and when Geoffrey arrived and the two of them went to dinner, Guy was nowhere to be seen. The following day she did see him in the hotel lobby, but Guy simply nodded courteously to them. Nearly all the staff and the other guests had seen her and Guy together, but no one said a word. Perhaps they were assuming that more had happened between them.

After the war Geoff took Lavinia back to the hotel for a weekend break. The staff pretended to remember them, and they managed to book the room they had shared on their last visit. Somehow, though, things were different. The place didn't seem quite so exclusive, and the quartet had dwindled to piped music. Peacetime seemed to take away some of the dramatic edge. There was a new Labour government, which had instilled a staid, austere attitude in the country. The hotel was still the same as it was, but it too had a grey, sombre tinge to it. Geoffrey even felt a little guilty when he ordered an expensive claret. As he poured it, Lavinia thought back to the time when Guy had ordered a pint of bitter and a pickled onion. She often thought of him. It was as though she had an entire lifetime of memories from just the one evening they had spent together, and even though the hotel had lost some of its allure, it was the thought of what might have been that gave the place a little magic. As if there were a corner of Lavinia's world that was independent and illicit, but none the less free of guilt. So much of loving someone means that you share all your secrets with them, but sometimes keeping something for yourself helps bind a relationship. If Geoffrey had known, there would be nothing for him to find out, no mystery.

In the sixties the old hotel was pulled down to make way for a car-park. On one of her final visits, Lavinia recognized a middle-aged woman working in reception as one of the girls from the quartet. While Geoffrey was taking an afternoon nap, Lavinia went down to the lobby and asked if she remembered Guy. The receptionist's eyes lit up, and her stern mouth curled at the corners.

'Poor Guy,' the woman said.

'Why do you say that?' Lavinia enquired.

'He was always alone. All the girls fancied him, but no one ever got close. We thought he was a queer.'

Lavinia felt herself blush. Her fantasy was crumbling. The receptionist smiled reassuringly.

'Then, one summer just after the war, Guy came here with a beautiful woman. She was in a wheelchair. She'd been some sort of ballerina, but she had been injured in an air raid. Guy had been a hoofer on the northern music-hall scene, but after his wife was crippled he vowed never to dance again. He was devoted to her. Smashing bloke.'

Lavinia remembered her night with Guy. 'But he did dance again?'

The receptionist shook her head. She was certain. 'No, he never danced afterwards.'

Had she not seen them that night? It didn't matter. Lavinia remembered, and somehow it was even more romantic now. She had kept her secret to the last, but now, with Geoffrey gone, there was no one to keep her secret from.

She gave Geoffrey's tuxedo to Oxfam. It would do for someone else. Afterwards she stopped off at Sagne's for a cup of tea. She started talking to a young man. She'd often seen him come into Sagne's for croissants, and he occasionally sat down for a cup of tea. She recognized Guy's flamboyance and Geoffrey's steadiness in him. He was the perfect combination of the two. He was muttering something, as if to a woman. Something in his tone reminded her of Guy, and she spoke to him. He was young, his life was ahead of him. She hoped he would find the perfect combination, balance out his own life.

∎

I had a break for a week,
So I booked my seat,
And confirmed a reservation,
At a quiet little seaside hotel.
I packed my bags,
And I caught my train,
And reached my destination,
Just in time for the dinner gong – ding dong.
Then I saw Lavinia,
Standing at the bottom of the stairs.

And I fell for Lavinia,
The moment that I saw her standing there.

Lavinia looked so divine,
As she walked up to the table to dine,
And then Lavinia's eyes met mine.

I thought can this be love,
Can this be lovey-dove,
Or just a holiday romance?
Can this be long-lost love at last,
Or is it just a flash in the pan?

Then after cheese and liqueurs they struck up the band,
I plucked up my courage and I asked Lavinia to dance.
That was the start of my holiday romance.
Just a holiday romance.

We did the foxtrot, samba and danced through the night,
The last waltz came and we held each other so tight.
That was the start of my holiday romance.

Just a holiday romance,
A simple holiday romance.
I wonder should I take a chance?

We walked on the beach,
And we paddled our feet,
And we watched all the swimmers,
And my holiday treat felt complete.
We drank lemonade,
And we sat in the shade,
I thought I must be on a winner,
And I acted cool and discreet.
For I knew that Lavinia,
Was the shyest lady that I'd ever meet,
And I knew that Lavinia,
Would only be my lady for the week.

HOLIDAY ROMANCE

It was just a holiday romance,
A simple holiday romance.
I wonder should I take this chance?
Just a holiday romance.

Can this be love,
Can this be lovey-dove,
Or just a holiday romance?

I tried to kiss her, she walked away,
She said 'Better stop, my husband's coming to collect me today.'
That was the end of my holiday,
Sweet and innocent holiday,
End of my holiday romance.

Art Lover

The blood was starting to flow from a cut over Lucian's eye. He looked at the knuckles of his right hand and saw the blood starting to form a bruise under his skin. His fourth and fifth fingers were swollen and distorted, and when he put them under the cold tap in the kitchen he thought he saw bone. He looked at himself in the cracked mirror. He didn't like what he saw.

When Lucian and Donna had moved in together everything was hunky-dory. Love in the afternoon, rolling over on the bare floorboards. Donna had snagged her ass on a nail, and they had both giggled as Lucian kissed it better. She had put blankets up at the window to keep out the light and make the bedroom more romantic, but the best lovemaking took place in the least likely places. Oral sex on the top deck of buses at night, and on park benches. The squat contained only the bare essentials for the lovers' existence: two mugs for tea; biscuits; toothbrushes in the bathroom. Now things were changing. Lucian's ex-wife had got custody of their daughter and was about to file for maintenance.

On the second floor of a squat just off Regent's Park, Lucian and Donna had been fighting tooth and nail. The kitchen wall was stained with red wine. Thrown by Donna in an argument. The rooms were furnished sparsely, with a mishmash of furniture, giving the impression that the inhabitants were not sure they'd be staying long. The door to the living room had been torn off its hinges during a quarrel about Donna having gone for a drink with one of her old boyfriends. The telephone had been ripped off the wall when Donna had woken to hear him speaking to his ex-wife in the middle of the night. In the bedroom a mattress had lain on the floor since Donna had overturned the bed with Lucian still fast asleep in it. Scattered around the apartment, scribbled notes. Vows never to repeat the violence. Promises to discuss things calmly in the future. Pledges to make amends. Hopes of starting again. Desperate messages of love. Reassurances from Donna that she would make more of an effort with his daughter. Reckless guarantees to marry when Lucian's divorce became final. Rash pledges of future happiness together. To have children of their own.

Lucian had been a member of a punk band in the late seventies. He'd been with Susie then. She had played bass and sung sometimes but it was Lucian who was the frontman. They had jumped on the punk bandwagon after the Sex Pistols had stormed London, but after a few gigs at the Roxy, they'd relocated and played the toilet circuit of seedy New York bars. They peaked in a support slot at CBGB's. But just as they were about to get signed, one of the band got busted, and Lucian and Susie were forced out of the States. Back in the UK, they'd had success with a cover of an old sixties song. Susie sang the lead vocal and became the focal point. The inevitable clash of egos followed, Lucian had broken up with Susie and left the band to concentrate more on his own songwriting. That's when he'd met Donna, in a coffeeshop in Marylebone. Donna stuck with him; she'd picked up the pieces and helped Lucian come back from depression. It had been a year since the band split, and Lucian's money had all but dried up. Then came the calls from Susie. She wanted to re-form the band, and Lucian reluctantly accepted. He needed the cash. Susie still wound him up, but Donna always caught the flak. Now the love-nest resembled a war zone. Lucian lurched into the hallway and said, deflated, 'This has got to stop. Nothing is worth this!'

There was no answer. Donna may have been unconscious, or hiding, but Lucian could not be sure. Maybe she was listening in through the intercom in the street below. She had left the entry phone off the hook. The buzzer rang and Lucian staggered over to reply. Before he could say anything he heard Donna's voice.

'It's me. If I promise to come back, you won't kill me, will you, darlin'?'

She sounded like she'd been sobbing. Lucian sighed and pressed the reply button.

'Look, I love you. This is madness. We can't go on fighting. Let's call a truce. My daughter's coming over Sunday afternoon. She can't see us like this.'

There was a pause. Through the intercom Lucian could hear the sound of a car driving by and children playing in the street. Finally Donna spoke.

'I'm going to the park to cool off. I'll buy you a cake on the way back.'

Donna would often go to the park to chill out after a domestic. An old bag lady often sat by the pond and Donna would talk to her, knowing that she would just sit and stare without comment or acknowledgment. Her silence made Donna feel secure, sane, that it was safe to speak her mind.

'My bloke and me. I love him like crazy but we always end up fighting. It's not healthy. One day, one of us is gonna kill the other one. Only gets to see his daughter once in a while when his ex-wife decides she wants something from him. Jesus, I hate blackmailing cows like her. No wonder he's driven crazy.'

Donna looked up as if something had suddenly become clear to her.

'I'd better get back. He needs me.'

The old lady just stared at the water. If she was listening she'd heard it all before.

On the way home, Donna stopped at a Pakistani supermarket and bought some almond slices as a peace offering.

Walking up the stairs of the squat, she could hear Lucian playing his battered old piano. His slow beginner's style – heavy on the left hand – gave the tune a tragic quality. She stopped on the stairs to pick up one of his shoes, which had come off during their scuffle. In the hall she picked up her underwear, ripped off during the fight. She walked over to Lucian and saw his bruised hands clumsily brushing the piano keys. His eyes were closed. A panel had been punched out of the bedroom door.

'This has got to stop, love.'

Lucian looked up. Exhausted.

'I know.'

Donna looked at herself in the broken mirror in the living room. Her blonde hair was hacked off close to her scalp. On the floor were scissors and piles of hair. She had sheared it off in a fit of depression. Lucian smiled, as if to approve.

'Looks brilliant. Like Joan of Arc, with attitude.'

Later, they walked hand in hand through Regent's Park and down Marylebone High Street. Their love had been restored. His anger at Susie and his ex-wife had mellowed. Temporarily. They walked past the pâtisserie where they had first met. Past the flower stall on the corner, towards a man sitting outside an antique shop and painting on a small canvas. He could have been a decade either side of fifty-five. His cropped hair was receding and going grey, and in his concentration he clenched his jaw, flexing a vein on his temple. His eyes glinted as he scraped away with a palette knife. He introduced himself simply as Fox. No 'Mr' or Christian name. Donna asked where he had learned to paint, and he replied in a word – 'inside'. After years in prison he was making the most of his time outside, taking in everything he could. Not a word was wasted when Fox spoke, as if every moment was valuable, as if he had learned to be reticent. If all his misdemeanors had been known, he would probably have spent twice as long as a guest of Her Majesty. He interspersed his words with the strokes of his palette knife.

'Seen you two before, ain't I? Like boats? Well, inside I never saw any boats, see. Bought a book, didn't I? Studied boats, I did. There. That boat there. That's a racer. A dragon. Never seen a real one, though. Did it all from my imagination. Kept me together while I was inside. I'd paint everything I saw. Anything I could remember. When I ran out of cons to draw, I started on things I'd never seen. Like that racer.'

Fox leaned back to take in the picture, at the same time checking for Donna's appraisal.

'Yours, love. For a tenner.'

Donna was sold. 'Done.' Lucian was not sure.

'You can't sell the picture just like that! Without any thought or feeling of attachment to it?'

Fox just leaned back.

'It's only a picture, ain't it? I think a tenner's fair. Any more would be takin' the piss. Go ahead. Can't hang on to it for ever. Maybe I can do you one day. Just take care you don't smudge it.'

Donna pulled out a ten-pound note and exchanged it for the painting. As Fox pocketed the money, Lucian felt that Donna had been conned. He could swear he heard Fox say something to Donna, and then laugh in a quiet, secretive way that excluded him. As they left Fox shouted out, 'See you, then,' as if he knew something about them. As if he had them marked. Another pair of mugs. The picture was a fair representation of boats sailing in a race, but Lucian knew it was tainted. It riled him that Donna liked it so much, and Fox riled him too. He was the real article, a tough old lag with a sensitive heart. The type Donna went for, the type he wanted to be.

Lucian had never been able to deal with rejection. He'd felt humiliated when his ex-wife and then Susie had left him, and felt the same now, as if Donna would leave him too. He brooded all the way home to the squat. Donna even bought him a cappuccino and an icecream from Bertorelli's, but he barely licked it before throwing it in the gutter.

Back home, Donna placed the painting on the shelf over the Victorian fireplace, then stood back to appreciate it, like a connoisseur. The bright colours shot out from the picture and seemed to turn everything else in the room black and white. Fox certainly had an eye for colour, and for detail. She could almost hear the sharp slap of the waves against the racers. The seagulls squawked and the wind blew against the mainsail. The vivid spinnakers leapt out ferociously. Fox may have imagined the scene, but when she gazed at the painting, Donna felt she was actually standing by the sea.

That night, Skin, their ex-drummer, came round with some grass and listened as Lucian played some of his songs on the ghetto blaster. Then he played a demo of a new song Susie had written. It was a soft ballad. Skin perked up when he heard it. Even he could spot a good tune. Lucian's face was contorted with anger. It sounded like a hit, but it wasn't his. His knuckles clenched tight. Skin took a puff of weed and made his exit. He knew the warning signs.

The pressure was getting to Lucian. He hated having to work with someone else in control. Travelling down to Cobham twice a week to the record producer's mansion. On his return to Waterloo Lucian was picked up in the manager's Rolls Royce and taken back to the squat off Regent's Park. Success was so near. Then just when it was within reach it was back to the ritual of signing on. The twilight world of living on the dole and waiting for pop stardom to return. Then the weekends when he saw his daughter. Those times hurt the most. That innocent six-year-old summed up all his lost hopes and failures, and all he held sacred.

Donna had been supportive at first, but he doubted that he'd be able to keep hold of her. Donna had qualified to go to university, and spoke languages. Everyone was attracted to her. That ex-con Fox had looked like he was chatting her up. Donna was the real thing. She was from Hackney. Perfect working-class credentials. Living with her, and in a squat, gave him some kudos, but he'd never be the real thing. He'd been privately educated by default, after being attacked by some boys at his school. His parents had divorced, and his *nouveau riche* father put him in a posh school in an attempt to drum some culture into him. He resented his father for that. The more desperately he tried to cover up his middle-class origins, the more fake, the less street cred, he seemed. Even his name sounded privileged. He would have preferred Sid or Jim, but he'd had a few hits as Lucian, and the tag was hard to shake off.

Later that night, Lucian phoned his ex-wife, and she demanded money for a school uniform for their daughter. Lucian tried to explain that he had no spare cash, but there was something in the pipeline. His wife hung up with a threat that unless he came up with some funds, he wouldn't be able to see his daughter the following weekend. The only thread of hope lay in the very thing Lucian despised the most. The band – Susie and the producer, who'd taken over his creative role. But it would be Donna who would feel the brunt of his anger. Once again, the meal she had prepared to soothe him ended up on the wall.

She ran out of the squat, and Lucian went back to the old piano. He started picking out that same little tune. A lullaby for something stolen. An opus to a wish that could never be fulfilled.

Donna went past the park bench where the bag lady sat and told the woman what had happened. How after all the anger she still loved Lucian. The ducks were hanging around like scavengers waiting for a tramp to fall asleep so they could steal his crumbs. A jogger ran past and the birds scattered, and their angry protestations echoed around the park. The old bag lady didn't even blink.

Donna left the park and made her way to the antique shop where Fox had been painting. Round the back to a small courtyard, she climbed the fire-escape up to an attic room.

Fox had done his best to make his little bedsit half respectable, but his years as a prison inmate showed. Newspapers and magazines were meticulously stacked in piles on the floor. Nothing was wasted or thrown out. Every inch of space was reserved for something particular. His few personal belongings were stored in a wooden tea chest next to his little single bed. The room had one window in the centre of the wall. The floor was covered in a cheap linoleum, with a slightly garish flower design, but a tiny Persian rug bought in a junk-shop gave him some comfort, some respite from the memories of a cold prison cell. Mod cons were minimal: a portable gas stove with two rings; a small refrigerator that looked as though it used to be a hotel mini-bar; and an old office lamp with a red bulb, which gave the room a hint of seediness once the sunlight had gone. Fox heard the church bell chime. Donna was supposed to be there now. He looked around anxiously to see if there were any last-minute adjustments to be made, and there was a gentle knock on the door. Fox received few visitors and Donna was the first woman to cross the threshold. He took a deep breath and sat on the bed with a pad, pretending to finish off a sketch.

'Come in, the door's not locked.'

Donna entered wearing a fawn-coloured Burberry raincoat. He did a double-take. She was wearing a black wig – along with black high heels and no stockings. It was a little chilly outside, and he could see the goose-bumps on her legs.

Fox thought it best not to comment on her hair, and tried to make her feel welcome.

'The kettle's on, would you like a cup of tea?'

Donna smiled gratefully.

'That's OK. I'd rather get started if you don't mind. Where do you want me to sit?'

Fox looked around, in a panic. He was unprepared and slightly nervous.

'Oh, on the chair by the window, to get the natural light.'

Donna didn't comment, and sat down in the chair. She took out a packet of cigarettes and slid off her high heels as Fox set up his easel.

'D'you mind if I smoke?'

'If you like, but it makes the continuity a bit difficult.'

Donna put down the packet and looked out of the window. As the light hit the left side of her face, Fox noticed a fading bruise, and found the position he wanted.

'There. Just there. Don't move. That's great.'

Donna didn't reply, she just carried on staring out of the window.

Fox tried his best to be professional, but he had never painted a woman before – let alone a real woman, and in his bedsit. He was just about to sketch an outline, when Donna startled him with a request.

'Do you mind if I take my raincoat off?'

Fox didn't mind.

She slipped off her coat, and her voice took on a slightly amoral tinge.

'I'm not wearing much underneath. In fact, nothing.'

Fox's hands started to shake, but he tried to stay calm, doing his best not to look at Donna.

'Just as you like, love.'

He looked at her. Her beautiful pale skin. Tiny hard breasts, long body with just a hint of loose fat around the waist. Then her legs. Still covered in goose-bumps and a few bruises along the shins.

'Get those playing football?'

'Just picked them up. You know how it is.'

'No, love. Don't know how it is. That one on your cheek must have been a real beauty.'

Then Donna took off her black wig.

'Excuse the disguise. It's a chance for me to be somebody else.'

Her short blonde hair seemed to transform her from a Latin tart into a Byzantine angel.

'My boyfriend thinks I look like Joan of Arc with attitude.'

Fox smiled.

Oh, he means Jean Seberg. The actress who played her. She was a goddess. My era.'

Donna smiled and suggested that Fox concentrate on her body. She parted her legs slightly, but Fox could only think about the gorgeous images projected on her luminous skin by those Rorschach bruises. Donna asked questions. Where was he from? How long had he been in prison? The only question he hesitated to answer was why he had been sent.

During a tea break, he did tell her – a crime of passion.

'Caught my woman with someone else and beat them both to a pulp with a cricket bat.'

Donna laughed. Half in disbelief, half in terror. Fox went on to describe the incident, graphically. The more it shocked her, the more lurid the details became. Eventually, he tried to justify his actions.

'I was drunk. Had been away for a couple of years and was let out on parole for good behaviour. I came home. There they were. Together. I just snapped, I suppose. The judge wanted me put away for ever, but they lived. I only rated GBH, so I got off light. I would have settled for double homicide, though. I wanted to do them both in. Still, I'm lucky to be out.'

Fox took a long hard look at Donna and asked about Lucian. Telling him, she realized how trivial her own situation was in comparison. Then he told her how he had used art as a therapy, to channel his anger into something beautiful rather than letting it use him to destroy and inflict suffering. Fox had borrowed a book on art from the prison library. When he talked about painting he seemed different. Almost scholarly.

'I was looking at the religious paintings. Della Francesca. The pictures were so calm and exact. All the perspective clinically worked out so that you felt detached from the suffering going on in the picture. Never related to that kind of thing before. When I first went down and got separated from the wife and kid, it wrenched me in two. Only violence and aggression moved me – Van Gogh's manic brush strokes, Goya's execution paintings. Then in a book I read about how to appreciate the delicacy of a curve or intricate shading, and perspective. It calmed me down. But nobody can ever get it quite right. I read somewhere that no artist is perfect. They search for perfection in their work.'

Donna was taken aback. She had no idea that Fox had so much feeling, let alone such an ability to articulate it. She found herself talking about the violence in her and Lucian's relationship. How the fighting was almost an accompaniment to their lovemaking. Fox smiled and told Donna to enjoy it while it lasted, eventually something would snap, passion that strong would envelop and eventually destroy. He also held out little hope for Lucian's kid.

'I had a kid with that woman I bashed up. There was no way an ex-con could ever get custody, so I just let it go. Your fella's doing nobody any favours waiting around all week for Sunday to come so he can pretend to be happy with his daughter for a couple of hours. He's just waiting for a kick in the balls. Kids can see through all those pretend smiles and that nervous laughter.' As for Susie and the band, Fox thought it would push Lucian over the edge. He didn't even have control of his art.

The session didn't last much longer; Fox explained that he could now complete the painting from memory. Donna felt she was being dismissed, but still there was relief when she put on her Burberry and left the bedsit. There was a strange clarity to Fox's thinking. So unsentimentally practical. Cut and dried, no frills. His cynicism had the opposite effect on her, though. She determined to make a real effort the next time Lucian's kid was down. She went into the bakery and ordered a cake so they could celebrate Lucian's birthday with his daughter that Sunday.

Back at the squat, Donna replaced a print which had been knocked off the piano. She rehung the framed poster from the Cubist exhibition at the Tate that covered up the crumbling plaster of the wall where she had smashed Lucian's Fender Stratocaster. Maybe they could take the child to an art gallery. Maybe they'd all find it soothing.

Sunday morning, and Lucian is walking through Regent's Park. There's a spring in his heel, as if he's entering into a new phase. He'd come to an agreement with his wife – he could see his daughter when it was convenient for her. He'd play the game and abide by the rules, take the judgement with a smile and accept that she had the upper hand.

He passed the old bag lady, sitting by the pond, staring into the water. He always acknowledged her, but he never got a response. Today, though, she looked up, and something in her eyes unsettled him. She broke the silence: 'Goodbye.' His mind began to race along with his heart. Any hint of friction, any false move. Any quarrel, missed meal, unjustifiable purchase. His daughter would be used as a spy. She'd report back. His wife would manipulate the information. He'd be at a disadvantage. That was the game they wanted him to play. Put him on the block and send him running round the track. It would be better to let his daughter go. No communication. Maybe he'd quit the band and he and Donna could make it work.

By now, he was slowly jogging back to the squat. He stopped by the flower stall outside the episcopalian church and bought Donna some flowers. He ran down the road, up the stairs, and burst into the squat to find Donna crouched on the floor. Her eyes were welling up with tears, anticipating the worst. Then she broke the news.

'Your wife phoned again. Your daughter isn't coming. She must have heard something about us. She said she'd call in a couple of weeks. How did she put it? Oh yeah, "when we calm down".'

They both sat down, too sad to be angry. Donna thought about Fox. She didn't dare tell Lucian about posing naked. Or about her new disguise. Lucian was thinking about the ex-con too. How art had helped him cope. His daughter was like a painting in a gallery. He could look at her sometimes, but she would never be his. And then there was his own art. Always angry. But the violence in his work had begun to take over his life. And all the time, there was Susie, knowing every emotional twist and turn. Feeding off his anger, invading his and Donna's life. When work and love got that entwined, the end was twice as bitter. Lucian sat down at the broken piano and picked out a gentle melody with one finger. All the anger had been punched out of him.

Sunday afternoon there's something special, it's just like another world,
Jogging in the park is my excuse to look at the little girls,
I'm not a flasher in a raincoat, I'm not a dirty old man,
I'm not going to snatch you from your mother,
I'm an art lover, come to Daddy.
Ah, come to Daddy, come to Daddy.

Pretty little legs, I want to draw them, like a degas ballerina,
Pure white skin like porcelain, she's a work of art and I should know,
I'm an art lover, come to Daddy,
And I'll give you some spangles.

Little girl don't notice me watching as she innocently plays,
She can't see me staring at her because I'm always wearing shades,
She feeds the ducks, looks at the flowers, I follow her around for hours and hours,
I'd take her home but that can never be,
She's just a substitute for what's been taken from me.

Oh, come to Daddy, come on.

Sunday afternoon can't last for ever, I wish I could take you
   home,
So, come on, give us a smile before you vanish out of view,
I've learned to appreciate you the way art lovers do,
And I only want to look at you.

Still Searching

My taxi turns the corner, and the driver points out the Tokyo Tower. 'It is 333⅓ metres high,' he says in broken English. I comment that it is like the Eiffel Tower in Paris. He asks how high the Post Office Tower in London is. Why is it that taxi drivers abroad can always chatter on in English, especially when I want peace and quiet, but whenever I get lost in a foreign city there is never an English-speaking person to be found?

I am in Tokyo to give a series of lectures on dream therapy. When I first started, in the late sixties, few people in the West took my lectures seriously. No accredited colleges offered courses in my field. I had no diploma. I simply gained my expertise by listening to people describe their dreams and watching their lives gradually unfold as the dreams became reality. I did attend a short course in alternative medicine at an evening institute in Ealing and lectures on homeopathy at a summer school in a battered old mansion just outside Ipswich, but I do not exaggerate when I claim to have become expert in my field by merely concentrating very hard and letting the truth happen. I was laughed at by academics, frowned upon by the medical profession and labelled a crank by the public. The only way I could practise my work was alongside fortune-tellers and bearded ladies at fairgrounds, and as part of the sideshows at county festivals. It was only when news of my therapy reached Japan that my work received some recognition. Strange, in such a modern, commercial society, but they have somehow held on to their beliefs. Now, I am one of the few dream gurus able to live from my practice.

I am checked into the hotel by my appointed guide, Dai. He has a round, generous face that always seems to smile, and while his English is not particularly good, he seems to understand everything I say. After handing me my room key and an itinerary for the coming week, he bows and wishes me a pleasant night's rest. He glances at the book I am reading. *Captives of the Empire*. On the cover there is an illustration depicting a Japanese soldier brandishing a large sword before a line of captive enemy. Dai gives an embarrassed smile, politely points out that the book has an interesting title, and takes his leave. I feel as though I have made my first mistake. The book was written by an older colleague who had been a prisoner of the Japanese in the Second World War, and I had promised him that I would try to find him a Japanese publisher whilst I was here. Looking at my itinerary, though, it is clear that I will have little time. Tomorrow I will give a lecture in the morning, do interviews and publicity in the afternoon and, after a short rest, a question-and-answer session, with readings from my *Memoirs of a Dreamer*. Even the evening meal is a business meeting with various representatives of the organizing committee.

The people here are very receptive to my theology. My Japanese sponsors have paid for my entire trip and secured me rooms in a large post-war hotel near the Tokyo Tower. But as soon as I check in, I want to check out. I complain to the front desk that my room smells of food and am informed that it is directly over the kitchens. The hotel is full but the receptionist promises to give me another room as soon as one becomes available. Meanwhile, I am given food vouchers acceptable in all the hotel restaurants as compensation. I am too tired to argue at this point and accept them. Before I go to sleep I glance through my colleague's book and read a chapter about the many prisoners of war who died of malnutrition working as slave labour for the Japanese building the Burma railway. I use my vouchers as a bookmark and fall asleep.

The next morning, I am woken at five-thirty by the sound of bells. My hotel is next to a large Buddhist temple, and the bells summon the monks for morning prayer. I get up and go for a walk to escape the aroma of fried Western breakfast which is beginning to permeate my room. It is a bright, crisp, sunny day. The clean winter air soon unclogs my nostrils, and makes my nose run. The stale air from my flight is finally starting to leave my body. My ears tingle with the cold, but I feel exhilarated. I walk into the park next to the hotel grounds and, behind a huddle of trees, I see the temple. Other tourists hover around the entrance taking photographs and speaking in hushed tones, but I walk straight in. Large black rooks perch in the high ceiling of the temple; a little man sits motionless in a kiosk. I leave, thinking I have to pay an entrance fee, but the man asks for nothing. Feeling rejuvenated by the atmosphere of calm, I return to the hotel for breakfast. As I enter the large breakfast hall, a crowd of people looks up towards me. They are there for my lecture. Part of my theology involves diet, and under these stares, I feel I must practise what I preach. I pass over the scrambled eggs and the hash-brown potatoes and settle for dry wheat toast, fruit and yoghurt. Then, nodding politely to my followers on the way out, I go straight to my room and order fried eggs, hash brown, a large pot of black coffee. I pay the waiter in cash so there can be no record of my purchase. With the vouchers the food is free but I am a prisoner of my own theology. I gobble down my breakfast and wonder what my followers would make of my deception.

My first lecture is well received, even though the audience is visibly taken aback by my aggressive performance. I'm well known for my laid-back oratory, but even though I try to relax, the caffeine rush from four cups of coffee over my secret breakfast has taken its toll and made my speech uncharacteristically shaky and staccato. I have lunch in the traditional, Japanese-style restaurant, then go to my room and take out a beer from the mini-bar. Alone, in privacy, I savour the alcohol as it immediately calms my system. That afternoon I feel refreshed and, with the aid of many bottles of mineral water, I breeze through the remaining obligations of the day. Afterwards I am a little troubled by my conscience. Surely anyone attending the conference would understand that from time to time I could have a fried breakfast or a tipple, but I feel as though I have let myself down. I feel self-protective, as if I'm open to microscopic scrutiny by my admirers. I finally persuade myself that my actions are justified, but at the same time I can't help feeling like a fraud.

I have finished my engagements for the day, but a group of delegates from Salt Lake City asks me to stop for a photo. I pose with a pretty young girl while her husband takes our picture. I am stunned when the husband encourages the girl to pose provocatively. At the last moment she pulls me towards her and kisses me passionately on the lips. I am flattered to find myself invited out by several groups of people, but it makes me feel uneasy and I explain that I'm tired and need to prepare for the following day. I return to my room, but once I am sure that everybody has left, I phone Dai and ask him to meet me downstairs in the lobby. I run down and jump into a taxi, in which Dai is already waiting. He shouts out our destination to the driver, and when I ask where we are going, he shows me a map of Tokyo and points to the Ginza district.

Dai is very aware of my sense of privacy and speaks only when spoken to. After eating a splendid meal in a smart Italian restaurant, I explain to Dai that I want to be alone to explore the district for myself. He gives me a very basic tourist map from the hotel, and after the customary bowing, bids me good-night. Over dinner I went to great pains to drink only mineral water, but now I am alone I feel it's safe to visit a few bars for Sapporo and chasers of sake.

Afterwards I stroll around, looking in the windows of the fashionable department stores and eventually I am drawn to a shop-window display of traditional Japanese goods. In the window is a life-sized mannequin, dressed in a deep-blue geisha costume. She looks seductive and elegant, with a grace that calms me and seems to separate me from the crush of the city. I'm back in the Heian era, when every detail had a meaning and people moved slowly enough to see it. Tokyo runs like clockwork, but retains an air of spirituality.

To my surprise I am joined by a young English woman, around twenty-three years old. She tells me about the geisha and Japanese traditions and when I ask her how she knows so much, she explains that she's a student of Eastern religion. We browse around the shop-windows. Everything is so expensive, but the Japanese seem to enjoy spending money when it is there. Like cherry blossom, money disappears as quickly as it arrives, and in some strange way there is a sense of relief when it has been passed on, a sense that it has obeyed the natural order. It's as if the people are in touch with something other than commerce, something more spiritual. *'Everything has a meaning,'* says the girl. Then she slowly walks away and disappears amidst the traffic. I dawdle outside a pachinko house. The Japanese go after work to play old-fashioned bagatelle. They hand over money in exchange for a bag of small silver balls, then play the machines with incredible ferocity. Their faces are animated, the whole place is buzzing with anticipation and activity. But the sound of the balls cascading around the machine cannot be heard, and from this side of the soundproof glass, it looks like a silent movie. I look at my watch and find that it's almost two-thirty. My first appointment is at nine the next day, so I hail a cab.

The door swings open automatically, and I get in. The driver speaks to me very politely in Japanese. (Where is my English-speaking taxi driver when I need him?) I try my best to communicate, but the driver scowls at the crudeness of my desperate finger jabbing at the red 'You Are Here' on my hotel map. Images of the Burma railway flash before my eyes. I immediately go on the defensive and am so suspicious that he will drive me all over Tokyo to maximize the fare that I pretend to recognize various landmarks as we pass them. The driver shouts out something. I don't respond. I think about my colleague and wonder how I would have coped as a prisoner of war. Then the driver repeats what he said. This time I pretend that I understand, and nod. He repeats it a third time. All I can muster is 'thank you' in Japanese. He smiles back and says '*arigato*'. There is an uneasy silence as he drives through a giant underpass. It reminds me of one of those labyrinthine tunnels the Japanese built for defence and for holding prisoners of war in South-East Asia, and I begin to panic. The driver seems deliberately to take me down the wrong street, and we end up getting caught in an endless maze of one-way streets. I shout to the driver in English. 'The hotel is near the Tokyo Tower, the tallest building in Tokyo, 333 metres tall.' I repeat this several times. It is my only point of reference. In his confusion, the driver pulls down a one-way street and collides with another cab. The two men wave their white-gloved hands around and shout at each other but, oddly, the incident still has an element of ceremony to it. Like two sumo wrestlers sprinkling salt and pounding the ground. Then they both bow and get back into their cabs.

My driver takes out some spectacles and reads the map intently. Eventually we reach the hotel and the driver points to the meter. Tens of thousands of yen. I immediately complain that he was the one who got lost, and we attempt a quarrel. We give up when we realize it's pointless. We can't understand one another's insults. He has picked up on my lack of trust just enough to refuse a tip, then I feel bad, ashamed of my panic, my suspicion, my lack of understanding of this culture. The days of wartime fanaticism are over. We bombed them. They rebuilt. No fault of theirs that they mastered their economy, copied and improved on Western goods until they outstripped our output and whetted our demand. I'm glad I own a Walkman and a Toshiba stereo. I suppose in this sense, Japan is the victor now.

Back in the safety of my hotel room, I quickly flick around the television channels – CNN and MTV. The local stations are just winding down. Although the language is alien to me, the delicate voice of the woman announcer puts me at ease. Soon I drift off to sleep, with the television still on, the voice of the television announcer in my subconscious. Then, in my dreams, I hear a woman's voice whispering gently in my ear.

'Everything has a meaning, there is a purpose.'

The message is soft, gentle; the voice friendly, reassuring; but at the same time I am filled with panic. I wake up abruptly. The television station has closed down. I fumble around for the remote and click off the television. My hotel room is silent apart from the low hum of the air conditioning. My head aches, and I walk over to the window to check that I've left it open. I have, so it can't be lack of oxygen. I look out at the Tokyo Tower, lit up nearby. Surely it will be time for the bells soon.

I ring down to the front desk and the receptionist tells me the time. It's only five. I lie down in bed, close my eyes, and wait. The bells sound right on time, five-thirty. It's a slow, deliberate, dull ring that resonates inside me. I think back to the taxi driver and that sad expression on his face. To how my own insecurity caused my suspicion and paranoia, and had made the unfortunate cabbie drive half-way around Tokyo and get lost in a city he knew like the back of his white-gloved hand. I wondered if everything had a meaning for him.

Tomorrow morning has all but arrived, and I have a busy schedule. I need to sleep and, in desperation, take a sleeping pill, but it doesn't work. I walk around the room. The left side of my body, from my shoulder right down to my ankle, is numb. I feel I'm going to have a heart attack. I start praying inwardly, God, please don't let me die in this strange place. Let my body wait until I get home. I catch myself, and start laughing out loud. Ridiculous to think such a thing. Then I hear the final sequence of bells from the temple. I won't go back to sleep now, and am drawn back to the temple. I gaze at the architecture and find myself thinking about the thousands of people who have sat here, considering life, wondering what it means. As before, I feel energized by my short visit to the temple and by the time I get back to my hotel I am ready to face the day ahead. I think of the English student in Ginza. Everything has a meaning.

When night comes I take a cab to look at the geisha in the blue kimono. Again her peaceful face calms me. After wandering around the backstreets I return to my hotel. There's a package for me at the front desk. I rush to my room, and like a prisoner of war opening a package from the Red Cross, I tear the wrapping away. It's a videotape. I play it, and find that someone has taped my movements from the previous day. It's me, I'm wearing the clothes I wore yesterday, but somehow I don't recall the movements. I am doing the same things but they look different, as if the whole thing has been acted out. Whoever made the video has cut it together so that my actions are out of sequence. It gives the tape an eerie, surreal quality. Various soundbites from my lecture cut together with conversations with other delegates rewrite reality in a peculiar way. At the end of the tape I'm walking in Ginza. There's a close-up of me drinking alone in a bar. Then shots of me in Ginza are cut with me kissing the girl from Utah. Surely it can't be blackmail? I suppose my conversation with the young English woman is used to assassinate my character further, showing me as a dirty old professor chatting up young girls. Sure enough, there's me looking at the geisha girl in the blue kimono. Then I see something that disturbs me. Or should I say something I do not see. There's no sign of the English girl. I can see my lips moving and just about make out the words, but it looks like I'm talking to the mannequin or, worse still, talking to myself. I rewind that section of the tape and play it again. Still no sign. I rummage through the wrapping and find a note torn from a yellow office-memo pad. 'Sometimes, dreams are more real than the world we know . . . Your devoted followers from Utah. PS We discovered this already on sale in a bootleg store.'

I feel as though I am being held up for scrutiny. Vulnerable and slightly paranoid. I can't work out how the bootleg was made. The street in Ginza and the street in the video were empty. If it meant being followed by secret photographers and having a false representation of myself sold as a bootleg, being a celebrity was not for me. I knew it had to be a fraud; I had many detractors who would seize the chance of exposing me. This trip is making me uneasy. That night, I make a substantial contribution to the hotel profits by finishing off the beer in my mini-bar.

Mercifully, the next day goes off without incident. The bells ring at five-thirty; I have breakfast in my room. I pay in cash. I steer clear of photographers.

Although I haven't had time to look for a publisher for my friend's book, I have shown it to a professor of psychology attending the convention. He explains that some prisoners of war coped with the crisis by going into denial, into a trance-like state. They lived, in fact, through dreams. Dreams had helped them survive, made them strong and able to cope. Their lives had been turned upside-down, the cornerstone of their civilization knocked away. Denied access to their loved ones, starved of hope, deprived of food and the basic necessities. Survive or die. Men thought at the time that they were behaving rationally, that they were in control, getting on with survival. After the war, they were unable to account for their actions at particular times, as if they had projected their minds elsewhere and blanked out reality in order to survive. It makes me think that perhaps I am in some sort of deep stress. My dream, the mysterious girl, is leading me to something I dare not face.

The next morning I wake with the sounding of the first bell at five-thirty. Without thinking, I make myself some green tea. I don't turn on the television, which at home would have been a habit. I just sit cross-legged, looking at the wall, gently sipping and contemplating the day ahead, the temple bells all around me. As the light breaks through, I decide to go for a walk. I pass the temple and take five minutes out of my day, just to think. The little man in the kiosk stares at the ground, still motionless. I walk up the hill behind the temple, past the beggars of Tokyo. Homeless people are everywhere, even here, a land that seems to have endless money and wealth. Looking down from the top of the hill, I can see a large golf range, astonishing in such a crowded city. Some early-morning golfers are already there, striking balls religiously. In the background, the Tokyo Tower. What a strange place this is. I feel an impulse to buy some gifts, presents to take home, even though I have three or four days left, and walk to a small shopping district. Most of the shops here are huge department stores, but I see one tiny bookshop that appeals to me. I am surprised to see that there are some books in English. I ask the girl if she has any books on Western psychology. She giggles, and pronounces 'psychology' in a strange way. She shows me a shelf where there are a few books – self-help books on how to avoid nervous breakdowns, etc. Even a book on the interpretation of dreams. I am amused to see that in the foreword there is a quotation from me. I thank the girl and say I'll be back. By the time I get to the hotel I'm already weary and my schedule has not even begun. My first appointment is an interview for a Japanese magazine.

The reporter has set up a small room in the hotel. I walk in wearily and think of Alec Guinness in *The Bridge on the River Kwai*, dragged out of his detention hole like a zombie, then staggering across the prison courtyard. A young Japanese woman explains that she will interpret for the journalist. He asks questions in Japanese. She nods, bows, asks me the question in English, then I reply and she translates back to him. A strange circle of communication. Suddenly, although the interview is very politely conducted, I start to feel threatened. I think about my colleague and his time in captivity here. What must it have been like to be questioned, examined, scrutinized by a stranger, and to be a captive of the Empire? The questions come sharp and fast. I start to hesitate and stutter; my usual confidence fails me. The interpreter seems to sense my difficulty, but the reporter keeps the questions coming, hardly allowing her time to translate. The girl is obviously embarrassed, but loathe to interrupt the interviewer, her superior. She bows and tries to compensate for my faltering replies, but the questions still keep coming, like an interrogation. She is trying her hardest. Here, everybody tries their hardest. It is a disgrace not to try your hardest. *Gambatte! Gambatte! Gambatte!* Somehow I manage to get through the interview, bowing, thanking, very polite, very civilized. I decide I need a coffee and go down to the hotel café. Lunch is starting, and the crowds are gathering, but a kind waiter shows me to a quiet table in the corner. My confidence is still shaky after the last few days. I came to Tokyo heralded as some sort of media star, in a glare of publicity. Now my faith in my work is shattered, and this makes me feel slightly fraudulent. The interpreter walks in looking tired and frazzled and somewhat bemused. She sees me sitting in the corner and is embarrassed. She feels disgraced by her performance at the interview, and I go to great pains to explain that I'd lost my concentration and that she shouldn't feel bad. She bows, thanks me, and leaves. Today there is no time for me to go on my pilgrimage to the geisha girl in the shop-window in Ginza. But the little bookshop is only two blocks away. The girl is standing behind her desk, and bows as I walk past. I have learned the custom and nod my head. The customer outranks the assistant. I browse through the books.

'You are searching still?'

I ask her to repeat the question.

'Searching, you are still searching?'

I am bewildered by her question and take it totally the wrong way.

'Searching for what? There is nothing to search for. I'm just looking for a few gifts to take back to England.'

'Yes,' she says, 'this will be good for you.'

She walks over to a section and pulls out a little book.

'*The Teachings of Buddha*. You look a lost soul. This will end your search.'

I smile. I was brought up Church of England, but took up Catholicism when I married. When I divorced I gave up on it but did not return to my original faith. I decided to rely on myself. As my work developed I took on board my own set of beliefs, and conventional religion had no place. But I've been caught off guard since I've been here. I think the bells from the temple have a lot to do with it. They ring inside me, disrupt the pattern I have made of my life. I have always been an early riser, able to concentrate on my work in the morning, but there was a time when I used to get up to think and contemplate, possibly to pray. The bells, the geisha, the English girl, the shop assistant – perhaps they pinpoint the dilemma hidden inside me. Embarrassed, I go to the bookshelves, pick up a few books at random, pay, and take them back to my hotel, along with *The Teachings of Buddha*. As I leave the shop, the girl bows again, saying something that perhaps she doesn't mean, doesn't even understand.

'I am so pleased your search is over.'

By this time I am late for my lecture. The hotel has cordoned off one of the restaurants to accommodate the audience of two or three hundred people. They are already seated, waiting patiently. I walk in with my books under my arm. The audience stands and applauds. I start my speech on stress and its relation to dreams, and the significance of dreams in the corporate world. The stressed-out business executives in the audience look as if they have never had a sober dream in their adult lives. Alcohol seems to be the only legitimate form of stress management in this country. Japan survives on stress. A very high suicide rate, fall-out rate, sickness rate, death by overwork. Success comes fast, but failure is waiting around the corner. My work in dreams focuses on stress relief, and this speech is the centre-piece. It's paradoxical that this lecture has coincided with the peak of my own unease. I'm flustered, but I must make the speech work somehow. I don't want to disappoint. I move towards the podium. Then I hear a voice.

'What is the point?'

Dai is whispering in my ear. What is he saying to me?

'What is the point?'

I look back at him and scowl. I'm about to start one of my most important lectures to date and my assistant is questioning its entire meaning, criticizing me, commenting on all I am. My nervousness turns to confusion, and the two of us embark on a farcical exchange.

'What is the point?'

'What is the point of anything? What do you mean?'

'What is the point you want slide to come?'

Once again I have misunderstood, just like I did with the taxi driver and the girl in the bookshop. I reassure Dai, saying I'll wave my hand and bow my head when the slides are due. These amateur theatricals get me through the speech, and for the most part the slides come up on cue. The audience applauds. I'm even asked for my autograph. It has been a success. Dai, my humble assistant, is almost crying with relief because he's tried his hardest, and succeeded. I compliment him.

'You have done well, thank you.'

He bows.

'*Arigato*. Thank you.'

I shake his hand, Western-style.

'You see. There is a point after all.'

We bow to one another, but he always manages to bow lower than me. On this occasion I agree. I am more important than him.

That night my left arm goes numb, my head aches. I am sweating all over. I take a few aspirin. My dreams are very confused. I think about my colleague, the prisoner of war. I'm being led past a row of shops in Tokyo. I'm put in a shop-window and displayed. Japanese file past and look at me inquisitively. I am being displayed as a criminal, an invader, someone with no respect for the people, their culture, their way of life. I wake up long before the bells ring. I go over to the pile of books I have bought at the shop and take out *The Teachings of Buddha*. As I open it the bells start to ring. Now I feel comforted by them. Like the girl in the bookshop said, perhaps I am still searching, perhaps I have lost my religion, my own sense of place in the world. Perhaps the bells mean to disrupt my pattern of life, to remind me that there is more, more than my own petty will to succeed. Everybody tries their hardest to succeed in this country, or they die or they are poor. It's the same the world over. But here people enjoy the moment. They are in touch with something past, something they are born with. The bells are friendly now. I turn the pages, read the stories. Everything has a meaning. Then I dream. I am walking along the tree-lined suburban street where I grew up in London. The oak trees form a massive arch. I seem to be in the distance and close at the same moment. I see the young woman I met in Ginza, but now she is wearing a long blue gown. She is joined by a man I recognize as my distant cousin. I haven't seen him since childhood. Now, the woman in the blue dress also looks familiar. When I am up close to them the woman looks at me and says something in English, but my dream does not allow me to understand it.

I wake on the floor. I've fallen out of bed. I've tossed and turned so much the sheets are soaking wet, and I can hardly breathe. My chest is tight and again I think I'm going to have a heart attack. I panic, but suddenly understand what the woman in my dream was saying. She was telling me to go home to comfort my cousin. His mother is dying. I will myself to breathe slowly so that I can control the pain in my chest. As soon as I am able, I phone my sponsor and explain that I must go back to England immediately. Waiting in my room for the taxi to the airport, I replay the video, still searching for the young woman. The front desk calls up. The taxi has arrived. Downstairs I take my leave of Dai. He tries to console me about my early departure.

'Everything has a meaning,' he says, echoing the woman in Ginza.

For a moment I feel I am not losing my mind.

In the cab I look through *The Teachings of Buddha* and make sure I haven't forgotten the bootleg video. Perhaps they have restored my faith. Clawed my theology back from worries of success and reputation, my dreams back into contact with life.

■

I am a drifter who has lost his way,
And I'm still searching for my dream.
A wandering nomad with no home to stay,
Just like a gypsy or a refugee.
Looking at another sign for another town,
Wondering if I'm ever gonna settle down,
Or am I gonna keep on searching till my dying day?
Still searching, still searching, still looking all alone,
Till I find myself a home.
Still searching, just like a rolling stone,
Destination still unknown.
When all my energy starts letting me down,
I get the feeling I'll still be wandering round,
Still searching, still working, still looking until I find a way.

The world is full of restless souls sleeping rough and living day to day,
Drifters who left families wondering why they went away.

Perhaps that's how I want to be,
While I'm searching for some peace of mind.
How can I find security,

WATERLOO SUNSET

A restless spirit who can't reach his goal,
Can't find a home until I've found my soul,
Still hitching rides and looking for a place to go.
Still searching, still working, still looking until I find a way.
I'm a drifter who has lost his way,
And I'm still searching for my dream.

Return To Waterloo

'God created man in his own image.'
— Genesis

Time passes, my dear clock-watchers. Time passes. The relentless tick-tock in my head tells me that it is time to begin another day. My creator, he who sees all, imagines he knows my inner secrets, but he is misled. I have misled him. Every day, he watches me as my train arrives at Waterloo and I disembark and make my predictable journey to my predictable day at Penbourne Estates. My wife Joanne is left at home in suburbia, in Guildford. My creator thinks that once he has extracted all the essence of my character, I will exist only as a flickering image on a piece of film passing through the gate of his editing machine. That my interior, my inner thoughts, the complexities of my character, are entirely of his making. Then he will replace me with an actor's face. But what will this man really know about me? Only what has been conveyed to him by my creator. My character has been given no dialogue. (The conceit of my creator knows no bounds.) He feels he can convey my story through looks and glances and the lyrics of his songs. The actions and reactions of other characters on my journey will be enough to tell my story. An audacious device, don't you agree, my old clock-watchers?

I was already in my creator's head when he pitched the idea of my story to the commissioning editors at the television film department. But my creator was in my head long before he thought he invented me. He will, in time, my old clock-watchers, recall how he was inspired by a pathetic commuter on a train journey to Waterloo. He saw me, his creation, crying. I was, in his words, 'sitting at one end of the carriage, holding a briefcase, and sobbing'.

How dare he assume he could possibly know what I was sobbing about? We never spoke or communicated. It was just a passing glance, and yet my creator actually had the gall to believe he could penetrate my inner thoughts and know everything about my life. Oh, the sheer boldness of it all, my dear clock-watchers. We all know that it takes more than a glance. But consider this. How many times have you looked at somebody just for a moment and imagined an entire catalogue of events built around them, constructed a complete character study based on that short, first impression?

But did my creator truly imagine me, or did I help him see his own dilemma? Was I a reflection of his own inner struggle? I may have been the one shedding tears, but he was the crying man.

I had seen him get on the train long before he would claim to have noticed me. He would often get on two or three stops after me and look for the most convenient seat, to write and sometimes sing into a little tape recorder without being seen by the other passengers. I am in my forty-third year and so, according to my daughter Lucy, I'm an antique. My creator is probably in his late thirties. I recognize him vaguely, a celebrity of some sort. Looks well for his age. But underneath that youth, I sensed that he was a man in turmoil. Caught in some strange time warp of his own invention. On one occasion I felt like speaking to him, but bowed to the custom of English commuters and decided against it. I was fascinated by the fact that he was obviously a man with little time to spare, but he did not wear a watch. He would refer to the clock on the platform as the train arrived at each station. As I studied him I knew this man, who would aspire to be my creator, was a walking time bomb, and using the turmoil in me to reveal the crisis in himself. It isn't until a clock-watcher sees another person's bomb counting down to zero that he acknowledges that this person exists at all. So, my tick-tock friends, let us observe our own accumulating countdown to catastrophe and, in the middle of it all, my creator.

A man who observes himself and the world around him as it runs out of time. We are all commuters on the train with my creator as we travel towards our Waterloo.

My obsession with women commuters began as a way of relieving boredom. The obsession became a compulsion and eventually my sole purpose for living. Then I found I had to turn what were, until then, fantasies into reality. To my surprise, my first advance did not result in a slap in the face, but in a caring, almost loving, hug. She must have been recovering from a broken relationship and I came along at just the right time. I never asked her name. If it had been allowed to go on, I'm sure it would have ended happily for us both. But she betrayed me. I arrived at our usual rendezvous at the Victory Bar, at the end of Platform One at Waterloo, and saw her talking to another man. It was probably an innocent conversation but my compulsion saw betrayal. A few weeks later, I was burying her body on a piece of waste land just outside Wimbledon. The following day, I went back to the Victory Bar and watched the man waiting for her. Time passed, as it does, fellow clock-watchers, until eventually he finished his pint of Ruddles and ran for his train.

My creator is a busy little bee, always making notes in his book, and sketches of other passengers. But unaware that in becoming so absorbed in me, I have absorbed myself into him, and he carries me with him on his own journey. (To think I thought my life was boring.) I must say that he has become quite obsessed with me. So much so that even when he stopped working on my project, I still lingered in his subconscious. These are the parts I enjoy the most. It's such a relief for me to use this person as a distraction from my own sordid little life. My creator and I would often take a taxi cab from Waterloo station to the West End. He is fond of walking around the parks of London. Mostly Regent's Park. He comes and goes. Occasionally he stops at telephone kiosks to make business calls. More often he is jotting down observations about me in his notebook. In the evenings I watch him as he takes a woman out to dinner. Attractive-looking, in her late twenties. She wears a Burberry raincoat, her long blonde hair flowing over her shoulders. I watch them dine; they talk incessantly. What a fool he must be to fall for a woman in that way. After dinner he makes a last-minute telephone call and comes back to the table looking relieved, relaxed, as if a great burden has been taken from his shoulders. But just when I think I can follow them home to the girl's apartment, he kisses her goodbye, jumps in a taxi cab and heads for Waterloo station. How I would have enjoyed following them into the apartment to observe their lovemaking, to listen to their pillow talk. Instead, I find myself on the last train to Guildford with my creator. That last cold journey back to my own unhappiness, disillusion and pretence. In these private moments he is unaware of me, which makes it easy to observe him. He takes out his notebook and starts writing romantic letters to his girlfriend. Childish promises, pompous statements, declarations of love. If only he knew he was missing the real story. My story. I could tell him so much, confess so much, inform him of the delights of being an invisible commuter. To be faceless, just another meaningless commuter.

In some strange, ironic way my creator inspired me. Watching him with that attractive girl that night in the restaurant gave me an idea. The following day, I went after the first woman I saw wearing a Burberry coat. She got on the train at Surbiton. It was obvious she got the train regularly, but for some reason I hadn't noticed her. This woman was not just a random target. This all had some meaning to it. I felt rather proud of myself. Liberated even. What could she possibly have done in Surbiton? What could anyone possibly do in Surbiton? It's just a stop-off. No one will miss her at Surbiton. It all seemed too easy. It was almost as if she had presented herself to me. She sat opposite me on the train, smiling at me. I tried to look embarrassed, but inside my feelings were much more turbulent. My creator was on the train. Got on at his usual stop. He looked a little worse for wear that day, as though he hadn't slept, as if he was under pressure. By the time we reached Waterloo, the woman in the Burberry coat was talking to me. Unusually relaxed, and very friendly for a commuter. We clock-watchers generally need a crisis – a war, a sporting event, something to wave a flag for – to bond us in some way. To my amazement, as we went through the ticket barrier, she actually asked me to share a cab with her. She worked near Somerset House by the Embankment, but for some reason I couldn't go with her. I made an excuse, although I could easily have gone. There was nowhere in particular I had to be that day. Why did I make an excuse? I didn't even want to join my creator. I ended up in Old Compton Street in the Pâtisserie Valérie. It was there I realized why I had decided to go no further. She had black hair. All the women who ever attracted me had fair hair, red hair at a pinch, but usually Scandinavian-blonde, flowing locks, like my wife and daughter. You see, continuing with this woman would have yielded no emotional satisfaction. I felt no connection with her.

One night as I was packing away a little bit of blonde crumpet into a rubbish bag by the line just outside Hinchley Wood, it occurred to me that perhaps my creator was a shadowing detective, obtaining information of my daily whereabouts. As far as I could gather, he only documented my movements during the day, as background, or a kind of research for my character. His idea of my life was a mundane drama-documentary. I now see that the character he imagines me to be is merely a metaphor for his own. My briefcase is his guitar case; he identifies with my outwardly respectable appearance. It's how he wants to see himself. All this nonsense he believes, that commuters like me have dull lives. If only he knew. Still, I'll let him impose his lyrics on my story, take me on his journey, and watch as the captives on the train pander to his imagination. But I won't submit. My will is stronger than his, my journey goes beyond his imagination. How surprised he would be if he had got the real story, followed me on my real journey . . .

Started off this morning as usual, in a panic because I'm scared of
   missing the train,
Another day, another journey, is it necessary or is it all in vain?

It is so long since I abandoned any sense of singular purpose, of
even the slightest desire to stand out from the crowd, that sometimes
I cannot even remember my own name. I have, in some strange
way, abandoned my own identity in order to become someone, or
should I say something, that fits into society. Let's just call me an
average commuter. My daily existence has become a montage of
simulated, obvious monotony. Almost as if each day is an action
replay of a life that belongs to somebody else. As though I move
from one scene to the next waiting for a greater being to breathe
life into me so that I can discover the meaning of originality. It has
been this way since I was born. Waiting for chance, praying for an
accidental encounter which might deliver me from my boredom.
Instead, I have found myself trapped on this journey. Isolated in a
train packed with commuters from Guildford to Waterloo, then
back again after work each night. Destination—terminal—death.
Depressing, you might say. Not really, my old clock-watchers,
merely the path of pragmatic realism. My creator sometimes busks
by the Underground at Waterloo and plays his little tunes from
memories past. The other day I swear he was singing a little ditty
about commuters, and I must admit the lyric struck a chord. As if
his words formed the soundtrack to my life.

Look at all the people around me, same old faces joining the queue

And every day I look in the ticket office with the same request . . .

For a return to Waterloo.

I liked that, clock-watchers. I could relate to that. Even the weather
forecast on breakfast TV this morning seemed to warn me not to
expect too much from the day. The forecaster's voice was unutter-
ably dull and uninspiring, as if to ward off any sense of excitement

or optimism that might still linger inside me. His tone was almost as condescending as that of an old schoolmaster who told me to expect disappointment if I applied for a certain job without the specified qualifications. Expectations of failure before hope of success. *But maybe today something special's going to happen, maybe this is my lucky day.* I caught a glance of my reflection next to a shop-window dummy and wondered if I was for sale, dressed in my conservative grey pinstripe suit, carrying my trivial-looking suitcase, whether anyone would bother to buy me, even at a knock-down price. Self-deprecating, my fellow time travellers? Merely factual, and very perceptive.

As I make my way through Guildford station, I see another woman. Sexy-looking, superbly built, with glamorous features and beautiful blonde hair. I am a little concerned, as it might be dyed, but she is too gorgeous to ignore. She's probably an executive secretary of some sort, and a definite cut above the norm. She looks to be in her mid thirties, a little mature for my tastes. Nevertheless, she will suit my needs until a younger candidate comes along. I can tell she's one of those flirtatious types who love to be stared at but at the same time make you keep your distance. Experience has taught me never to make small talk with her type. She could cut me off with a glance. I'd turn violent and attract attention. No, playmates. I'll bide my time.

She stops at a newspaper stand and, to my surprise, buys a tabloid newspaper. Why would she want to look at bare-breasted sluts on page three? Is it meant to excite me? To delude me into thinking she is promiscuous and lift my expectations, only to give her more satisfaction when she finally humiliates me? I would enjoy dealing with her, my old tick-tock watchers, revel in her initial look of disgust, stifle her screams and squeeze out the look of fear in her eyes.

Out of the carriage window I see a group of schoolchildren getting excited as they leave for a day out. The train pulls out of

Guildford station, and I feel a spark of optimism run through my veins, as though each journey signals the beginning of a new life. My journey will take just under an hour, adequate time in my isolation cell to ponder my life of bad luck and misfortune. If this sounds a little pathetic, please forgive me, my old cell mates, for I speak only from life's bitter experience.

The children run up and down the platform, and the young woman teacher is finding it difficult to control them. That's it, little young ones. As long as you run free there is hope that you might escape. Ah, the sound of innocent schoolchildren at play takes me back to my own schooldays. What times.

I think back to that time long ago, when youthful exuberance filled my body and my mind was free of pressure to succeed. Before school, and competition. The chase. The race. The victory. A or B stream. Qualifications. Class. Accent. Background. Breeding. Success. Status. Autocratic despots laying down the law to destroy ambition and preserve the pecking order. Beaten on to cattle trains, and into servitude. Exaggerated, you might proclaim, my old commuterites. This may be. But in the darkest corner of your own tiddly-wink, my dear accomplices, surely you cannot deny my claim. Were you elbowed out, held back, incapable? As I sit in my tight little seat in a crowded train I want to cry out to the world.

> Somehow I feel the world has been passing me by
> Can't help feeling somehow I've been living a lie.
> When I was young the future was clear it was easy to see.

But now I am here. I just want to be free, and every day I wonder.

> Will I reach my destination? Or will I get lost along the way?

I shout out inside but no one can hear. It's not a question of actually getting lost. I am here and lost at the same time. And there is no doubt about me reaching my destination – I'm on a return journey, I'm going nowhere.

Have I stopped or am I only going slow?
Have we got a couple more stations,
Or is this as far as we all go?
The headlines cry out from the papers,
Inflation, murders, war. Who really wants to know . . .

Why is it that even though I buy my own newspaper, I am still more interested in what the man opposite is reading? 'SURREY RAPIST . . . ANOTHER VICTIM'. The police have intensified their search for the man . . . mid forties . . . well-spoken . . . do not approach . . . extremely dangerous. Twaddle, twaddle, blah, blah, blah. What do they really know, my fellow partners in crime? Zero is what they know. There is even one of those ridiculous-looking Identikit pictures of the rape suspect that could resemble anyone in the world. Even me. I do wish for once that the bloody tabloids would get the facts straight. How do they know I am well spoken? None of the victims could have told them. Not to say that I am not well spoken. That is beside the point. But I would like to point out that I am not always dangerous. It is only when necessity demands. So far, I would say that all the girls have found me to be remarkably mild-mannered – as rapists go. The tabloids should add 'MURDERER' to the headline.

Somehow 'RAPIST' looks trivial beside that rather misleading cartoon of my face, but still. It doesn't suit my plans to be apprehended immediately. I will decide when I will be caught. If ever. My mind drifts from the photofit image, out of the carriage window, to the pretty school-teacher on the platform. Her flowing fair hair reminds me of my own dear daughter Lucy. I imagine my Lucy turning and looking at me the same way she did that summer evening, when I observed her naked in her bedroom. It was accidental, but the look she gave me made me feel dirty – guilty, somehow, of invading her privacy. Shortly after that she left home. Without warning. I hope she didn't leave because of me. My wife always said I had a look in my eye sometimes that seemed to terrify her.

Like a shark ready to strike. Merciless and cold. Lucy had become such a beautiful seventeen-year-old. With our only child gone, my wife and I realized we had only each other, and reality became unbearable. Our lives were, in effect, over. There was no more love. No more communication, or understanding. Only guilt. Fear. Passion suppressed. Distrust. That awful embarrassment whenever I showed any physical affection. Intimacy is now only a word, something we shared many years ago, before Lucy was born. As for sex, she recoils as if I am some kind of ogre, 'I'm not the same person she fell in love with.' That is nonsense and she knows it. Once she would have joined in my fantasy and indulged every whim. Without her, I'm alone, on this train alone, but liberated by the possibility of an affair with any woman who takes my eye.

There are three businessmen sitting opposite me. All three wear the same uniform. Pinstripe suits (blue, of course), white collar and tie. A typical cast for one of my scenes. I plot out their lives and gain the one thing I do not have in my own life. Total control.

The tall, thin, constipated-looking one is so finicky he holds his newspaper away from his face, as if it has a rare disease. He is probably an accountant or a banker, plays bridge, goes grouse-shooting with his chums and screws his wife at 11.45 every Saturday night. The 2.2 children both go to boarding-school, which he can just about afford, and he probably wets the bed worrying about how to keep up with the Joneses. Poor pathetic bastard. The little chap in the middle, just got on the train, late for his first day at the new firm. The stupid twat is reading a book on chartered accountancy to impress his new employers. Sad little cunt. He'll soon learn the ropes on the ladder of success.

Now the race has begun, you are strong and you are young.

He'll probably fall in love with the receptionist and get married, just so he can look back in years to come and say he trapped himself.

Then, because they know he is vulnerable, the firm will embrace him and elevate him to assistant to the underwriter's clerk. He'll have to suck his boss's dick for a rise of fifty pence a day. He'll take on a mortgage he can't afford to please the blushing receptionist bride, and after a while he'll lie awake at night. Premature ejaculation. That cold sweat afterwards. Counting the debts, the grey hairs on his temple.

> Stand in line, join the queue, play the game with the right
> attitude,
> (It's your chance, it's up to you, be good to us and we'll be good
> to you)
> And you will be rewarded for conforming to our plan,
> The system will accept you, because we understand.
> You'll be up there with us achieving the best,
> WINNING, CLIMBING, ON THE LADDER OF SUCCESS.

The fat, sweating chump in the aisle seat, reading his smart, trendy novel, is undoubtedly a tax inspector of some description, going up to the City to bankrupt some unfortunate hard-working devil.

> And your efforts will be noted,
> You always must compete,
> Stick it out, the sky's the limit, and you'll be part of the élite.
> You'll be up there with us, competing with the best,
> Achieving, winning, on the ladder of success.

As I watch these three characters in my play, I realize that in them I see the beginning, middle and end of my own career. The optimism of the young hopeful, seated between anxiety and complacency, defeat and success. I could shout out loud that it was all a lie, he should get off at the next stop and run, not journey to Waterloo. He wouldn't listen. He will go to his own hell and play the game.

> Make commitments, join our scheme,
> Now you're really one of the team.

Until they decide to kick you out.

> Part of the plan, don't make a fuss,
> Play the game and you'll be one of us.
> And your efforts will be noted,
> You'll be part of the élite.
> Take your money, make your choice, now your commitment is
>   complete.

That's what happens. They make you buy into the whole idea, then they beat you to death with it.

> Stand in line, join the queue, play the game with the right
>   attitude.

Don't you dare to answer back, my boy, or you'll find yourself on the dole queue.

> Now you've made your reputation, there's so much that you can
>   lose,
> It was a struggle to get up there, you've really paid your dues.
> Now you're up there with us, competing with the rest,
> Winning, climbing, on the ladder of success.

No, nothing can be done to alter this young man's journey. The same as my journey. It was inevitable that I should reach this point of no return. Do not cry for me, dear commuter. I am quite happy to accept my destiny. That busker is strumming my life.

> Will I reach my destination?

I will, my old clock-watchers. Undoubtedly. I will.

As my train pulls into East Horsley, I see another pretty young girl. Just like Lucy. A delightful young flower being sent off by doting parents to the cultural and historical spots of London. Or so the brazen little cow has told them. She is going up to King's Cross to sell her arse to some Arab pimp. Oh yes, definitely Arab fodder. The peaches-and-cream complexion. Frumpy sports jacket, obligatory Walkman playing inane, juvenile pop songs, pouting red lips and cropped blonde hair. Definitely worth a Middle Eastern grope or two, I'd say. I think I'll follow her to King's Cross. I'll pose as a potential client and take her to one of those cheap hotels and strangle the little bitch. But not before I've had my money's worth. I'll slip out of the front door, down into the Underground with all the other worker ants. That's the joy of being anonymous. No one will remember me. No one will see me. Even my wife would find it difficult describing me to the police, the amount she's looked at me in the last few years. Ah, now the young fledgling is speaking to Mummy and Daddy, telling them not to worry. How considerate of her. Even if they never see her alive again, they'll have the comfort of knowing they said goodbye. More than I had with Lucy. It was as though she just disappeared. We contacted the police, but after an initial spate of concern, their interest waned. They put her on the list of missing persons, and they left us alone. The irony was, old chums, that the police wanted me to make an appeal on television. Well, you can imagine what a dilemma that put me in. No chance of showing myself on television, particularly knowing what I know. I decided to let it be. I explained to my wife that it would be best to keep the pressure off Lucy, that she would contact us when she felt ready. A few weeks after she went, I got into my office and was surprised to find she had left a message on my answering service, saying she was well and not to worry about her. Not to worry. Try telling that to my wife, my old clickety-clicks.

She left her message after the tone,
I hear it over and over on the Answerphone.
No one can find her address unknown,
She just decided to go out and make it alone.
Solo, solo. My little child is going solo.
I feel like crying, I'm in a rage, can't understand why she just
    went away.

165

What made it happen? Guess we'll never know.
She just decided to go out and make it solo.

Now the train is pulling away, and the concern on the faces of both parents is clear to see. They probably think that she will be back in two weeks, just like she said, but until she returns home safely, there will always be that lingering doubt. Is it not poetic, my travellers in crime, that I am the only person in the world who can put my hand on my heart and honestly say, unless I decide otherwise, they will never see their daughter alive again? The parents are deep in conversation.

We work like dogs all our lives,
Like millions of other husbands and wives,
Sent her to college, didn't care what we spent,
Think of how we feel, she didn't say, she didn't ask, she just
    went.
It's like a pattern, it's like a crime,
We see it happen time after time.
You raise your children, you watch them grow,
Then one day it's goodbye, they've decided they're going solo.

The little frump is sitting down at the end of the carriage. Look at Lady Muck. She's just lit up a cigarette and now she's reading *Cosmopolitan*. She does remind me of Lucy though. Especially when she smiles. It's odd seeing it all from this perspective. After seeing both the parents, I can understand why the girl is relieved to be getting away from it all. It's sad, but all they'll have to remember her by will be those old family snapshots. Thinking of snapshots, I was amazed at the way, almost overnight, Lucy turned into an adult. One day she was a playful little child in my arms, then she grew breasts and started to get coy in my presence. I tried my best to put her at ease, show her it was only affection I had for her, but she would start to turn away whenever I tried to grab her for a kiss and cuddle. It was embarrassing, a little humiliating.

The toys are forgotten now, it appears,
They've let you down after all of these years.
You sacrifice all, now there's nothing to show,
Ungrateful youth has decided to go it solo.
The obligations and all of the ties
Have got to be broken so that they can survive
Just because you give them life, you can't stop them grow
Can't hold her back now, she's going solo.

I saved that message Lucy left and play it every day when I get to work. I imagine that she's just called. Telling us not to worry. Giving us all her love. If only poor Lucy knew that all I ever wanted to do was to give her and her mum all my love. At supper, the Grand Canyon separates us, not the kitchen table. There is nothing worse than nothing. Lucy pulled us together, but now, the sadness is awesome, the grief total and unrelenting. Is it not paradoxical, my fellow psychic explorers, that even I, with my dark, concealed inner world, can experience such anguish? Is that what drives me onwards?

I overhear two old ladies sitting in the seats next to me. They're talking about some chap similar to me. That poor fellow lost his job, but in order to keep up appearances, he pretended to go to work every morning and spent all day walking around Hyde Park. Came home in the evenings and talked to his wife as if everything was normal. One day, he left and never came back. It's intriguing to listen to random conversations. Sometimes, because they tell you what you want to hear, you can draw some parallels with your own life. Trouble is, with my straying eyes, I get caught staring. Now one of the old dears suspects I might be giving her the eye. I think she actually called me a pervert. Never mind. A cheap thrill never did anyone any harm. I must be careful not to blow my anonymity. It will only take one person who remembers me. I must withdraw inside myself. Have less and less to do with the world until I cease to exist. Someone else is staring at me. A mouse-faced woman. In an Eastern bloc country she'd probably work for the secret police.

She's got the newspaper with the Identikit photograph on the front page, and I swear she has seen the resemblance. After shuffling around in her seat, she looks up at the emergency cord. For a moment my paranoia starts to get the better of me. I try to remain calm but my blood is boiling inside. She looks at the newspaper, then back at me. Then I glance down at the headline. I could have written it myself – about my Lucy.

> Have you seen this face?
> Does it ring a bell?
> Does it strike a chord somewhere in your mind?
> And there's a big reward, if you help us solve this crime.
> And if you recognize this face, dial 999.

. . . But the last thing I can do in my situation is go to the police. I would only incriminate myself. I would become the hunted one. If I made just one mistake the whole jigsaw would fall into place . . .

> Have you seen this face, dig deep in your mind.
> Has anybody seen that little girl of mine?
> She was always a rover, but I'm afraid to say she strayed too far
> this time.

My wife has probably put two and two together already, but she is too terrified of me to spill the beans and go to the cops. That's why I must go home every day. So she doesn't have time to build up the courage. On the other hand, she's desperate. So beside herself with worry she can't think straight. For all she knows, I've got another woman. Perhaps I've lost my job and am covering up, like the unfortunate man the old ladies were talking about. But my wife worries most about whether I molested her Lucy, driven her away. No, it would serve no purpose, explaining to my wife. In any event, she would never believe me. Best leave her be, with her coffee mornings and aerobics.

Now I'm sitting at home, staring at the wall,
Waiting for that missing person to call,
Waiting for the message I'm dreading to hear, waiting to confirm
    my darkest fear.
She's a missing person, and I wish I could see
All of the places she might be.
Maybe I stopped her from being free,
Maybe there was something missing in me.

How would I react if Lucy was dead? Faint? Throw up? Start to
weep and fall into my wife's arms? Would it bring us together if
we knew, or drive us apart for ever? How would I feel if I saw that
sad little body lying in a mortuary? It is all too sad to contemplate.
But at least we'd know for sure instead of living on false hope for
the rest of our lives. She'd no longer be on that endless list of lost
faces on police files, no longer a statistic.

Wherever she is, I hope she's doing fine,
But I wish that she would phone or drop a line.
Till then I've got nothing to ease my mind,
And I'm thinking about her all the time.

I suppose if I had the choice, I'd give myself up if it meant that
Lucy could come home. You see, my friends, I am not without
feeling. I too have a conscience.

Now, thank God, that wretched mouse-faced woman has got
off the train. My conscience is guilty, and troubled. She's still
watching me as we pull out of Effingham Junction. She'll call the
police as soon as she finds a telephone. For a moment I consider
getting off the train myself, but that would only cause more alarm.
I must continue with my usual routine and hope that I'll be protected
by being just another commuter in the crowd. Safety in numbers.

Cobham station. For a moment, I can forget about my problems.
The gentle purring of the train's engine instils a feeling of calm.
Even the thin, constipated-looking commuter opposite looks at

peace with the world. He even manages a slight smile as a bird sings in the distance. The tranquillity makes me feel almost proud to be English, and I consider myself extremely lucky to be part of such a genteel well-mannered nation – for an instant. A ghetto blaster bellows down the corridor of the train. The young thug carrying it is a skin-headed punk dressed in obligatory black . . . A rather attractive punk girl is with him – also in black, but a tight sweater and mini skirt. She looks very sexy, but behind all that face powder and red lipstick, I suspect she's ridden with disease. With them is a slimy-looking youth, dressed more up-market. This punk's hair is slicked back like Al Pacino's in *The Godfather*. Too many movies, young man. He's a slimeball of the first order and makes no bones about despising everybody else on the train. In many ways, as much as I dislike him, I empathize with this. He resembles me in that sense alone, but if I had my way, I'd have him and his kind stuck up against a wall and shot. Doubtless, he would have me suffer the same fate. They've upset the silent status quo, and as Skin turns up to full volume, he looks over at Slick for approval. My only conso-lation is seeing the look of irritation on the face of the fat chump opposite. The little trainee accountant next to him probably likes the music, but is too terrified to show his approval and incur the wrath of his pinstriped travelling companions. The situation is flammable. At least these noisy degenerates have stolen some of the attention from me. This comforts me slightly, but then the ticket collector comes. In my panic to keep out of the spotlight, I fumble through my pockets, and for a moment I can't place my ticket. The fat pig opposite smirks as I start to grope through my clothes. He would like me arrested and imprisoned for mislaying my ticket. I wonder what suffering he'd inflict if he knew the real extent of my crimes against humanity. Then – eureka! – I find the ticket. To the chump's annoyance, I settle back in my seat.

Out of the ghetto blaster an unsingable anthem of chaotic caco-phony. A song about the world selling them out. No dreams or ambition left. The punks think they're original, but it's the same old complaints.

> You sold me out to get a better deal for yourself.
> You sold me out, and now we want some of your precious
>   wealth.

As they sing along, it hits me inside – it could have been me who betrayed them. But we've all been dragged into the double standard of eighties culture. It's no fault of mine that to survive on the ladder of success I too have sold out my fellow countrymen. They'll do the same one day. It's the natural way to survive in this world. I sell off my country to rich foreigners when I should help my countrymen. But it's not my fault. The guilt hits and humiliates me, as Skin groans off key.

> Work all your life, put the money in the bank,
> Sign the dotted line.
> When you try to draw it out, the joke's on you, they put up the
>   empty sign,
> 'Sorry mister, we're all sold out.'
> You sold me out, to get a better deal for yourself.
> You sold me out, but now we want some of your precious
>   wealth.
> Got no dream, got no ambition, can't decide 'cos there's no
>   decision,
> Got no claim to any position, can't compete with the competition.

Their grotesque, bitter mutterings are almost touching in a simplistic way, and then it hits me. They could have been me. Their reality could have been mine. Lucy is of their generation and probably feels like them. But I can't tolerate Lucy feeling the same way as these people, following the same fate. My emotions run rampant as the punks shout at me.

> You sold me out. Sold me out.

The almost violent despair in their voices provokes such hatred inside me that I start to tremble with anger. I fantasize about brandishing my briefcase and using it as a weapon of destruction. Suddenly I lose control, and in one swoop decapitate Slick, and then the constipated businessman, whose head rolls on to the lap of the young accountant next to him. I break Skin's neck, but he falls over still clutching his precious ghetto blaster. Now I have found an outlet for my frustrations, I inflict fatal wounds on all the commuters in striking range, but even though the bodies fall at my feet and the heads roll on the floor, I can't stop that music. I can halt the machine but can't stop the noise.

Reality snaps back and I find myself shaking in my seat. Thank God the tape has stopped. I am reunited with that soothing suburban calm. I close my eyes and pray. What have I done? I must remember to remain calm. I open my eyes and breathe a sigh of relief. The carnage is in my head.

The train pulls in at Claygate station. Desolate suburbia. A couple of middle-aged ladies get on with an old woman. She's blind, but her sunglasses make me suspicious. I have to see the eyes to know she's blind. Surely she can't be on the look-out for the Surrey rapist? No, that would be too melodramatic. The girl punk says she'd rather be put down than be as old and helpless as the blind woman. Skin guffaws moronically. Slick sits back and considers the conversation. He looks like he'd have a few ideas for getting rid of the old and infirm. Skin looks at the front page of the newspaper the mouse-faced woman left behind. He laughs at the Identikit picture. Says it looks like his dad. The girl pouts and studies the picture. She says the man looks sexy, then takes a bite from a large green apple and smiles at me.

I'm almost flattered by this last remark. It's an artist's impression of me, after all. If it wouldn't give me away, I'd almost introduce myself. Then Slick picks up the paper and sneers at the photofit.

'You know what I'd do with people like this? I'd put 'em against a wall and blow their bloody heads off.' He grins sinisterly, as if threatening to do the same to anyone on the train who got on the wrong side of him.

The train starts up again, wobbling from side to side. I'm trying to keep myself to myself, but the girl is giving me the eye. She takes off her leather jacket, staring at me the whole time. Another police trap? My ego gets the better of my caution. Next moment she's standing up in the aisle beside me pulling down her little leather skirt, which has slipped up her thighs. Incredibly no one else seems to notice this. As she makes her way down the carriage she looks back and gestures for me to follow her, and I have to pinch myself. Am I day-dreaming? This is real. I wait until the girl disappears into the next compartment before getting up to follow her. I am still concerned about attracting attention and I'm careful not to disrupt the other passengers, but decide that if the girl is genuinely attracted to me, why not enjoy it and arrange to meet her somewhere after the journey? If, on the other hand, it was a police trap, I'd simply say it was what any middle-aged man would do in the situation.

I reach the door to the first-class compartment and see the girl waiting at the other end. I know this section of the train will allow me a certain amount of privacy with her and proceed with more confidence. She smiles again before disappearing into the toilet, and I hurry along to join her. I can smell the trail of cheap perfume. Usually I have to make the first move, but her advances, out of the blue, have given me a real blood rush. By the time I reach the door, the girl is already seated on the toilet, her leather skirt up to her waist, her bare legs straddled over each side of the seat. For a moment I try to back out, but the girl reaches forward to drag me in. I stand over her, and she stares up at me, running her tonguearound the inside of her open mouth. I hear the sound of trickling water as she urinates. She flushes the toilet but stays seated, relishing the cold British Rail water as it splatters her. As she reaches over and unzips my trousers, I double-check to see if the door is 'Engaged'. Suddenly I wince with pain as the girl squeezes my genitals. Before I can react she has pulled herself up by my necktie, and sticks her tongue into my mouth. I can still taste the citrus from the green apple on her breath as she starts to suck my face. Some of the red has disappeared from her lips. (I must clean myself up afterwards.) The girl's wet bottom is protruding over the edge of the basin and one of her legs is cocked. Are you watching, my old tick-tock compatriots? She rubs her face on my chest, and I slip my hand under her crotch and start to play with the wet patch between her legs. Surely, my old clock-watchers, if all women were this provocative, there would be no possibility of rape. Surely then the world would be a better place? Suddenly I think of Lucy. I remember the night I burst into her room while she was standing there naked and that look of shock on her face. My wife's look of disgust when she watched me innocently cuddling her daughter in the back garden last summer. Embarrassment and guilt make me cringe and I yell out. The girl has squeezed my balls and twisted them around in my underpants. She bites my bottom lip and spits in my mouth. Laughs in my face. I imagine my Lucy doing the same. Mocking me. The girl sneers and runs out. I see myself in the mirror – dishevelled, ashamed and humiliated.

Are you watching, my partners in time? Do you feel what I feel? Look at my sad face, covered in lipstick stains. Do you not think it makes me look like a clown? Is it any wonder I do what I do? This continual humiliation at the hands of women has driven me to the edge. I wash and brush up, and regain my poise. But the short walk back to my seat lasts an eternity. People are talking about me.

'He's old enough to be her father. He should be ashamed of himself.'

'I had him down as a trouble-maker as soon as he got on. I'm going to complain to the authorities when we get to Waterloo.'

I'm paranoid. They don't speak. They don't even notice me. Like all good commuters.

But the punks don't play the game. I get to my seat and encounter real hostility. Skin watches me sit down, calls me a 'stupid prat' and turns up his ghetto blaster. The girl takes out another apple and winks at me, while Slick just stares at me without blinking. I suspect that, like me, he will wait for his moment. If anybody else on this train is trouble, I'm convinced it is him. He reaches into his inside jacket pocket and pulls out a comb, and before running it through his hair, points it at me as if it were a gun and pretends to blow me away. I remember his threat. 'I'd put 'em against a wall and blow their bloody heads off.'

It's at times like this, my tick-tock friends, that my ability to disappear inside myself provides the most comfort. I imagine a calming, gentle place where my loving wife sits in a quiet English garden at sunset. She's a picture of serenity as she sways from side to side, cradling my darling infant Lucy in her arms. As I lay down on the rolling lawn, I close my eyes, and the delicate smells of flowers fill my nostrils. In this vision of paradise, I hear the soft sound of a piano. My dear wife kisses me tenderly on the lips, and together we sit on the grass, while I hold our baby daughter.

Darling, I am so afraid,
I know I should be strong, but when affection is gone, it's hard to
 face each day,
Knowing love has drifted away.

I look up to see the young businessman getting off the train at Surbiton. It's probably where I should have got off all those years ago. Maybe he did realize what he was heading for, and decided to get off the train before reaching his own Waterloo. On the other hand, maybe Surbiton was as far as he could go. Poor chap. Two elderly men get on the train. Relics from the Second World War quite probably. They're both in civvies, but their rank is defined by their manner. One is a major, sprightly and upright, with a clipped middle-class accent. The corporal shuffles humbly along beside his superior. It's amusing to see them still living out their rank even though it is nearly fifty years since either of them saw active service. Ironic, isn't it, how my ambitious youth got off when old age got on? Something inside me wants to call my wife, to confess and ask her forgiveness, but at the last moment, something holds me back. I must continue with my journey. There is no turning back. Through the window of my carriage, I see the face of a stranger. It is not until I manage a smile and he smiles back that I realize it's a reflection of myself. How strange it is to see myself as part of this play. Through the reflection I see a young woman in dowdy clothes with two children. One about eight years old. The other an infant in a pram. The woman cannot be more than twenty-five but a hard life has aged her. Seeing her makes me shudder with anger. Whenever I see young women like this, I'm always reminded of my mother. The eight-year-old could easily be my older sister. She ran away from home because she was afraid of my father. I was lucky. Too young to remember. But she was old enough to see the fights, to recognize abuse. Mum was one of those stubborn loyal types, standing by the old man when my sister ran away and not hearing a bad word against him even after he died. Always making excuses for him – the war, unemployment. I suppose the scars from the beatings healed and she loved the old bastard. But what about us kids?

'Surbiton. This is Surbiton. The train on Platform Two will call at Wimbledon and Waterloo only.'

The whining, sharp, female voice of the announcer erupts in my ears. It's annoying, but comforting to know that through all my inner tumult order is maintained in the railway schedule. A train passes in the other direction, and the announcer's voice is muffled. She sounds like my wife, her voice cracked with emotion.

'This is Surbiton. Surbiton . . . for anyone who is there, after eighteen years of happily married life . . . about a month ago our daughter left home and since then . . . I am beginning to suspect that my husband is seeing another woman. Lately, there have been secrets between us . . .'

The announcer snaps back into a more formal voice.

'This is Surbiton. Surbiton.'

I have a quick look around for my wife, but I know my imagination is running riot. My eyes settle on a man sitting reading the newspaper in the waiting room on the platform. He looks up at me, doing a double-take. Our eyes meet, and I quickly look the other way. It's only a matter of time before somebody recognizes me. Time is running out.

The train pulls away. The old men sit down just in front of the punks. I wonder what they make of the world. Britain must have been a much more powerful nation when they were young men. It's fascinating to think that a whole cross-section of society is represented by passengers on this train. Society needs all types. It needs opposition, conflict. The old soldiers hate the unruly punks, who mock the old-age pensioners, who are shocked by promiscuous women, who detest the businessmen, who look down on everybody else. Even murderers and rapists have a role to play in a cruel, obtuse way. Society needs something to hate and fear. A common enemy. Much the same as Hitler was. It draws everybody together somehow and breaks down all those barriers between us in the comfortable eighties. The old soldiers made me remember how much I loved the idea of the British Empire when I was a youngster. How I looked up to the servicemen who saved us from being overrun by the enemy in the two world wars. Now all people have to unite them is their hatred of unfortunates like me. Punks, old soldiers, scared housewives, bankers and old-age pensioners. In me they all have a point of convergence. Someone to despise and focus their distrust, unhappiness, recrimination and anger. As long as my image appears in the public consciousness, that someone is me. A common enemy is vital. How else can you know that you are not the enemy? Even when I get the maximum penalty, I won't complain. I'll fall on my knees and thank my accusers for giving me such an important role. It's only a matter of time before the old soldier starts to complain about the noise from the ghetto blaster. I'll sit back and watch the drama unfold. It's going to be fun. Neither side will back off. I must steer clear of any controversy and remain anonymous. I will simply act as impartial observer. Instead of acting out my own fantasy, I will watch as the world entertains me and life's melodrama takes centre stage. Strange, though, that in each player I see a part of myself. They are all me.

The lighting is right. The ensemble complete. The principals in place. The train at full speed. Let the opera begin.

OLD SOLDIERS and MIDDLE-AGED LADIES
What has become of this land that I fought for, this country I served with
  pride?
It is sad that the good times have gone, and all of the good men have
  died.
Every man for himself, that's the motto,
What has this great nation become?
All the violence and lack of respect for us by almost everyone.
See it dying, see it fading, see it drifting away,
It is over and forgotten, now they'll throw it away.

The MAJOR*'s lips are tightly pursed, his eyes bulging with pent-up anger as he looks over at* SLICK, *wishing he could put the young upstart through some square-bashing.* SLICK *looks back defiantly.*

OLD SOLDIERS and MIDDLE-AGED LADIES
Young people today are a positive shower,
Can't imagine how it all went wrong.

The GIRL *is bored by what she hears. The same propaganda has probably been drilled into her by her parents.*

OLD SOLDIERS and MIDDLE-AGED LADIES
And who will inherit the mantle of power when all the great leaders have gone?

SKIN *leaps up on to his seat, turns the ghetto blaster up to maximum volume and thrusts it in the face of the* MAJOR. *You can see the reaction on the* MAJOR's *face, but his frail body has already fought its great battles, and there is no energy left. The* OLD SOLDIERS *can only look on defencelessly at the cruel pantomime and make pathetic protests.* SKIN *presses 'Rewind', and an excruciating noise screeches around the carriage. The* BUSINESSMEN *look up in horror.* SLICK *looks around the carriage and cynically shouts at the passengers.*

SLICK
'Cos the system that bred you and fed you will throw you away,
And it's not far away.

SLICK *jumps up and grabs the* SEXY SECRETARY, *who is innocently sitting in the row behind. His moment has arrived. The train careers around a bend in the track.* SLICK *and* SKIN *are now both on their seats, holding the ghetto blaster triumphantly as it plays their anthem of hate and destruction. They are joined by the* GIRL.

OLD SOLDIERS
The modern youth will ruin the nation.

PUNKS
Not far away, not far away.

OLD SOLDIERS
Signal the end of our civilization.

PUNKS
Not far away, not far away.

The BLIND LADY *looks tense and afraid as she rubs her arthritic knee.*

BLIND LADY
I feel it in my bones,
Gets worse every day.

SLICK *and* SKIN *jump over to where the* BLIND LADY *is sitting. They push* FAT PIG BUSINESSMAN *to one side and shout in the* BLIND LADY*'s ear.*

SLICK and SKIN
The future is here,
And it won't go away.

While SLICK *and* SKIN *terrorize the* BLIND LADY, *the* GIRL *vents her anger on the* FAT PIG BUSINESSMAN. *She sits, legs astride him, and rides him as if he was a wild animal, tugging at his hair, slapping his backside and punching his fat jowl.*

BUSINESSMEN
Total chaos, total destruction,
Social collapse, moral corruption.

The PUNKS *jump on the* BUSINESSMEN *and start beating them up.*

PUNKS
Not far away, not far away.

The OLD SOLDIERS *look on helplessly as the* PUNKS *continue their assault on the* BUSINESSMEN. SKIN *grabs hold of* CONSTIPATED BUSINESSMAN *and smashes his head against the window of the train. The sounds of the blows to his abdomen and of his skull being pummelled against the glass augment the stomping music from the ghetto blaster.*

OLD SOLDIERS
The empire is dying, see our heritage crumbling.
We didn't ask you to stay, so will you leave us alone.

SLICK *runs to the end of the carriage and reaches in his pocket. He takes out a revolver and waves it around, terrorizing the passengers.*

SLICK
And we'll segregate the people according to their race,
And no one's gonna listen when you try to plead your case,
And those who think they are secure will get slapped in the face.
Chaos will rule, no one will be safe, the ending is near and it's not far
   away.
The future is here and it's ours to dictate, the ending is closer so why
   hesitate . . .

The PUNKS *now stand above the others on the train.* SKIN *walks down and forces all the passengers to their knees, as if to prepare them for an execution-style shooting.*

BUSINESSMEN, OLD SOLDIERS, MIDDLE–AGED LADIES
The empire is dying, but once it was great,
Someone must do something before it is too late.

In all the confusion, the PUNKS *have forgotten the* BLIND LADY. *Seeing her,* SKIN *walks over and takes off her dark glasses. He backs off, a look of horror on his face. Her eyes are missing. Before he can move away the* BLIND LADY *reaches into her shopping bag and pulls out a kitchen knife. She rips into* SKIN'*s guts, then his face.*

I use the diversion to escape from the carnage. I remain the silent majority. A time bomb waiting to explode. In a perfect fantasy, I would be the one to stand up and save society from these evil punks. But no. My instinct is to run.

Yes, my fellow tick-tock people, a somewhat extreme catalogue of events, I'd agree. The action may be dramatized, but it does reflect a society such as ours *in extremis*. We have been trained to stifle our instincts, to bury them inside. They fester and rise and explode.

The train seems to build up speed as it enters a tunnel, the clattering of the train over the rail tracks shudders my sensibility so that my entire nervous system goes into trauma. My fantasy play mingles with my own nightmare scenario. Remorse at the loss of my daughter, compacted by the guilt of deceiving my wife. The faster I go, the further the tunnel seems to extend; the more I try to separate myself from the past, the more it rears up in front of me. The world is closing in and I am trapped on this relentless journey. A day excursion speeding on a collision course with my own past.

I see faces from my youth, the schoolteacher who smothered my ambition. My pitiful attempts to better myself, only to find that man can go only so far on the ladder of success. The eventual compromise of living out in the suburbs in more affordable surroundings. Working hard in a job I dislike, selling valuable properties to the rich and powerful when so many of my countrymen live in squalor. My sense of betrayal as my beloved country finally discarded me. My desperate attempts to restore a relationship with my daughter. My crimes against humanity. Confused faces at the moment of violent death. All the passengers on my journey close in like the walking dead, and among them I see my wife holding Lucy, telling my infant daughter that one day I will abandon them both. Again in the darkness of a tunnel, I see myself on a giant television screen, portrayed as the Identikit rapist. Hell descends. I'm in an empty hospital, searching for my daughter. I see her in the distance and start to walk towards her. She's sitting up in bed brushing her beautiful blonde hair. I get within touching distance. Lucy turns and smiles. But the relief is blown away by a gigantic gust rushing along the tunnel and pushing me against the wall. I turn to see Lucy laid out on a marble slab in a mortuary. Her body dissected by a pathologist. Her beautiful hair matted. Her limbs contorted and bruised. I'm both the bereaved and the murderer.

The train gently leaves Wimbledon station. Past the rubble on a building site. As my journey continues, the daylight lifts the gloom.

Is everyone around me on a journey towards their own Waterloo? Perhaps mine will end sooner than most. I can still hear that busker, singing the soundtrack.

Will I reach my destination . . . or will I get lost along the way?

I open my briefcase and take out a batch of keys. They open the doors of a sumptuous mansion, for a wealthy Arab sheikh. I'm handing it over, selling off my country to the highest bidder, maximizing the sale, but losing the investment in my own life . . . Soon we will pass Vauxhall, my birthplace, and a tenement called Coronation Buildings, where I grew up with so many ambitions and so much faith in the country that bred me. I'll die for my country, but as a traitor.

> Now all the lies are beginning to show,
> And you're not the country that I used to know.
> I loved you once from my head to my toes,
> But now my belief is shaken.
> And all your ways are so untrue,
> No one breaks promises the way that you do.
> You guided me, I trusted you,
> But now I must awaken.
> Thought this empire would be here at least a thousand years,
> But all the expectations and aspirations slowly disappeared.
> Now all the lies have gone on too long,
> And a million apologies can't right the wrong.
> Soldiers die, but the lies go on,
> But now we must awaken.

Through the streets of industrial London, where as a boy I watched the trains to Waterloo pass me by. I always promised myself that one day I would be on one of them. I got my way, but the train brings me back.

We had expectations, now we've reached as far as we can go.

Approaching Vauxhall station the train slows. The station is decorated with Union Jacks, streamers, bunting. It's empty, but there's an air of celebration.

> And all your manners are too too polite,
> Just to prove that your conscience is whiter than white.
> You had your day so get ready for the night,
> For another dawn is breaking.

Past the archaic Victorian wrought-iron girders. The slow turning of the wheels against the rusty track echoes in the giant cavern of the station, and I know that this is the past that I have never left. On the platform I see a boy waving at me, and I recognize him as myself. I lean with my arm outstretched and drop the keys to the future in the palm of his hand. He grasps them tightly and clenches his fist in a promise never to let them go.

> We had expectations, now we've reached as far as we can go.

The other passengers haven't moved. They're still in the same position. There's an atmosphere of tranquillity as we make the final turn into Waterloo. The punks have turned off their ghetto blaster. The little fair-haired girl from East Horsley is still smoking a cigarette in a non-smoking section of the train. One of the middle-aged women is describing the view of the Houses of Parliament to the blind woman. The old soldiers are discussing the way the London skyline has changed over the years, and Slick takes out his comb for a final run through his greasy hair. The sexy secretary straightens out a small crease in her jacket while the fat pig opposite checks his watch. And what of me? I've hardly been noticed. The girl can barely look me in the eye. And the other commuters? How surprised they would be at their contribution to my journey. How shocked when they realize they have been travelling with such a wanted man. I think back to the busker in the Underground.

> Will I get away, will I see it through on a return to Waterloo?

Disembarking, I see a policeman standing at the end of the platform by the ticket collector. At the barrier, behind the policeman, there is an Identikit poster of the Surrey rapist. I pass quickly, but a voice tells me to stop. I turn around expecting handcuffs, but it's only the ticket collector wanting my ticket. A feeling of relief numbs my body. Freedom has been granted for one more day.

Still, the clock is ticking and time waits for no man. There is much to attend to, my weary travelling companions. A sense of urgency returns, bordering on panic. A new subject! Then, through the mêlée of humanity, I see the frump from East Horsley. I follow her down into the Underground. The Underground, my place of worship. My home. You see, clock-watchers, there is an evil spirit that lurks in the Underground. South, north, east and westbound. It hangs around in dark corners, waiting for the sign of an inner weakness. A lonely heart, a desperate soul, a troubled mind. Then it musters its predatory power when a train rushes through, rushes through to a lost man with an innocent stare before it takes its prey and swallows whole. The subway of the spirit is looking for a messenger to carry its dark madness obediently to the light to spread and spread from man to beast, from fish to fowl, the madness. Open the wound, transmit softly on a spoken word. It has always been there.

Principal photography is now finished and my creator feels very pleased with himself. He is cutting fragments of me, and as my image flickers slowly through the editing machine, I turn and look into the camera, at my creator. I stare into his eyes and study him. So much has happened in both our lives since we first encountered each other. He has moved out of his house and shacked up with the young tart in the Burberry raincoat. She's cut her hair. A change of image. She's left her boyfriend in the squat. Says he was violent. It was all romance and shagging to begin with, my old clock-watchers, but now – blood has been spilt. She's brought her anger with her. Tried to attack my creator with the bread knife. He's just as bad. Breaking under the pressures of this project, no doubt. Or is it that he has discovered something of himself in me? If he ever topped her he could always call me as a character witness. But who would believe me? I'm just his invention. An image on film.

My creator leaves me stranded at Waterloo at the end of his film. Without wasting your time, my dear clock-watchers, and I do admit that this has taken a little time, my character is a sad, ineffectual man, crushed by the world, elbowed out, held back, incapable. He was only let travel so far, around and around on a return to Waterloo. The end, you may say. Not I.

The camera is reversed. I haunt my creator. He cannot sleep. He knows he has missed something. He keeps playing a scene over and over. A scene shot in a dark tunnel, with me and the girl from East Horsley. In his mind he walks into the tunnel, turns the corner, and a gust of air rushes underground and connects his thoughts with mine. It carries with it all the silent screams. He's jarred out of his sleep. He has to shoot a new scene. Has he found me out? But how can he change his story now? My mundane drama-documentary has become surreal. In the new scene I'm walking towards my creator, down that Underground corridor, him strumming a guitar like a subway panhandler. Will he denounce me? I prepare myself for the worst. Face to face, he stops playing and I stop dead in my tracks. We stare at each other. The true test. But my creator is weakened. The gust thunders through the subway once more. It takes both of us with it to hell. I suck my inventor in through my eyes, absorb him into me and carry him with me on my journey. He can no longer denounce me. He is condemned.

Afternoon Tea

Mementoes of past relationships punctuated the room. A small painting of yachts sailing in a harbour; a cracked teapot shaped into a man's face, the lid moulded into a rock 'n' roller's quiff, and two cups and saucers in the same style; a poster from an exhibition of Expressionist artists at the Tate hanging tentatively on a small nail over the fireplace. Several girlfriends had come and gone, each leaving behind something for Lucian to remember them by. When the relationships were solid and the feelings were strong, these items would be treasured, but when the relationship was over they would be left to the dust with an almost masochistic relish.

Donna had been the last to split, almost two months ago now. Their favourite records, and photographs of them together were still scattered about. Some of her clothes hung in the closet, and more were still in her suitcase, never unpacked, as if she always knew she would leave. There was a pile of unopened mail in the wire mailbox inside the front door, mainly bills. Lucian was interested only in personal communications. Perhaps Donna would change her mind, write to him, come back?

Lucian walked from room to room. The place was untidy; he'd long given up cleaning. It was becoming obvious that the occupant was living alone. There was a pile of dishes in the sink; his clothes were strewn around the floor; empty beer cans littered the kitchen. The only semblance of order was a neat row of cups and saucers on the kitchen mantelpiece over the stove. Three times a day Lucian would go through the ritual of making tea. It was in childhood that his love of the ritual had developed. He had watched his grandmother prepare the Sunday tea – salad sandwiches, watercress and spring onions on thick-buttered doorsteps of farmhouse bread. Grandad would bring in some fresh tomatoes from the greenhouse and take a pinch of salt from the condiment tray and sprinkle it generously over the open sandwich before closing it shut. For afters, fruit cake, still hot from the oven. It was the familiarity of the ritual that calmed him. Not so much the smell of the tea, the taste of the cake, but what it gave him. The chance to stop in an ever-changing world and consider the moment. It was there that Lucian's fascination with cake had also begun. The addiction had started.

Lucian liked to have breakfast at the Sagne Coffee Shop in Marylebone High Street. Sagne's had been there since the twenties. The current owner, Sidney, wore a starched white jacket, like a doctor, and treated his guests like family. Lucian could easily have picked up the cakes for tea when he bought his breakfast croissants, but somehow that would have spoiled the ceremony. Sidney always kept a few chocolate cakes aside for when Lucian called in at about three-thirty. He still bought two of everything, maybe thinking of happier times, with Donna. The smell of freshly baked cakes wafted in the air, a sweet delight, a smell of optimism. Nothing escaped Lucian's eager gaze – the Danish pastries, sticky buns, the Battenburgs. Sidney automatically put two fresh croissants in a bag, and Lucian gave him the right money.

'How's your luck today? If you're like me, you can't complain. I could have sworn you were going for the chocolate croissant this morning.'

'You know me, Sidney, I'm always loyal to my croissants in the morning, but, who knows, one day I may surprise you.'

'Will we see you at teatime?'

'Work permitting.'

The way Lucian spoke it was obvious there was no work, but Sidney kept the conversation upbeat.

'Try to come in if you can, I'm putting a few new cakes on display. Just trying them out, to see how they go.'

'You're tempting me again, Sidney. You know I can't resist.'

Sidney gestured towards an empty seat.

'Sit down, I'll give you a sneak preview.'

Lucian sat down at a table, next to a well-groomed, affluent-looking woman – at least seventy, but she'd kept herself well. Still a glimmer in her eye for a man. She looked at Lucian coyly, almost like a teenager. He looked around, remembering the time when Donna worked behind the counter, the first time they had met. Donna would watch him as he gazed, mouth watering, upon the rows of cakes – the cinnamon rings, chocolate éclairs, the Danish . . .

Sidney emerged with a cake, temptingly concealed under a serviette, and presented it to Lucian with a flourish. He sat down and leaned forward conspiratorially, all the time keeping one eye on the customers, like a spy passing top-secret information or a drug dealer closing a deal with a desperate junkie. His voice dropped to a whisper.

'A layer of marzipan as the base . . . a few soft, ripe raisins . . . another layer of moist, paper-thin pastry, another layer of marzipan, vanilla custard, topped off with a fine glaze.' He looked into Lucian's eyes. He knows his client is hooked. 'I can bring you a strip if you want. Go on, try it. Try something different. You won't be disappointed.'

Lucian tried to resist, but the temptation was too much.

'OK, you've got me. Let me have it.'

He had taken the bait, but he knew he would not be disappointed. Sidney never overpitched his wares. If cakes could be compared to women, then this was a complete seductress. Lucian was tempted; he would resist the moment and prolong the pleasure. Oblivious to the woman opposite, he thought of Donna and spoke in a low, sensual whisper.

'There, my little work of art, I'll take my time with you today.

There is no rush, my sweet thing. My mouth wants to eat you, but my lips can only say that I adore you.'

The old lady looked over at Lucian with understanding.

'Don't worry, my boy. It's just a piece of cake. Enjoy it for what it is. I often ask myself, are cakes masculine or feminine? Generally, the latter. Rock cakes, they should be men, but éclairs, truffles, petits fours, no, definitely feminine.'

Lucian was concerned. Was she all right? The old lady continued, politely, matter of fact.

'It's such a pity to eat them, though, because when they're finished, what's left? Nothing. The taste lingers for a moment, and then – only a memory. So I say, just be grateful you enjoyed it while it was fresh and new. There will be many more for you to enjoy. My late husband and I were great cake lovers. My husband always maintained that there was nothing more civilized than tea and cakes. Geoffrey preferred tarts. I used to tease him about that.' She could see that Lucian was slightly unnerved by her story, but went on with it nevertheless. 'Do you have a favourite? The Danish too rich for you? Find a cake that will suit you – not too sweet, not too rich. Somehow things haven't gone your way, but one day you'll find perfection.'

Lucian paused for a moment, thanked the old woman, took his croissants, and left. He felt strangely optimistic. Was the old woman trying to tell him something? Lucian plunged into Baker Street tube, ready to embark on an orgy of pastry shops, and memories.

The journey from Baker Street to Hampstead took only twenty minutes. He was soon back in one of his favourite student haunts, back in his European period – the paintings, the cafés, the pastries, the girls. He went into Louis's and ordered a chocolate twirl. He thought about Jana, a first-generation Yugoslav, his first love. They had met at college. There was an aloofness about her that must have come from old Eastern European ancestry. Long, high cheek-bones, broad pouting lips, fine brown hair. Mondays, they had always ended up in Louis's. Talking music, art, politics, revolution. Walking on the heath. She would kiss him on the face, spontaneously, for no apparent reason. Rapid kisses in a patting motion. Not erotic, but affectionate, full lips exploding into a small popping sound every time they connected with his skin. Nostalgia. Sentiment.

He got back on to the Tube and made his way down to Soho. He strolled up Old Compton Street, past the porn shops and cafés, the restaurants, oriental supermarkets, soaking in the metropolitan atmosphere, avoiding the alleyways where danger lurked. He walked past the Pâtisserie Valérie two or three times before plucking up the courage to go in. It was lunchtime and the place was full, buzzing with loud, aggressive media types, foreign accents, attractive women with rich, older men.

He had a piece of Madeira cake, and was reminded of Doris. He'd met her in a dingy club in Wardour Street when he was a student. She'd worked as a prostitute and used to go down to the club to listen to Lucian's band. She was two or three years older than him, and knew much more about the world. Sometimes they'd go to the Bar Italia, but it was in the Pâtisserie Valérie that they really felt at home, at the little corner table in the back room. She was rough trade, he knew, but honest through and through, and soft, sweet and sympathetic. Sometimes she would crumble, like a Madeira, and Lucian would try to protect her, take her away from the prostitution and pornography. But there was no way she was going to change.

He moved on, and again got caught up in memories. He'd taken Doris to Fortnum and Masons, for afternoon tea, but they had looked down on the poor art student and his battered piece of crumpet. So had the Ritz. They'd ended up at Lyons tearoom just off Trafalgar Square, drinking milky coffee and eating jam doughnuts. Afterwards they'd sat by the fountains in Trafalgar Square, facing the National Gallery. Lucian had wondered if one of his pictures would hang there one day. He'd been a rebel then, trying to create fine art that satisfied politically as well as aesthetically, fancied himself as an avant-garde artist whose work would buck society – if society would dare exhibit it. Now, instead of feeling spited by the art establishment, oppressed by his tutors into producing pretentious tripe for café society, reinforcing the status quo, he recognized his own work's crudity. Maybe Donna had been too much for him, too rich in layers, like the Danish. He'd have to learn to live alone, to cater for himself. He thought of Donna's clothes, still hanging in the closet on a rusty rail. She wasn't coming back. She'd left after that last quarrel, with only the clothes she had on – a skimpy summer dress, high heels and her old Burberry raincoat. She'd been different for some time. Now Lucian realized. She'd been going to meet somebody else.

■

Tea-time won't be the same without my Donna,
At night, I lie awake and dream of Donna,
I think about that small café, that's where we used to meet each day,
And then we used to sit a while and drink our afternoon tea.

I'll take afternoon tea if you'll take it with me,
You can take as long as you like because I like you, girl.

I take sugar with tea, you take milk, if you please,
I like you talking to me because you ease my mind,
Afternoon tea, afternoon tea.

Tea-time still ain't the same without my Donna,
At night, I lie awake and dream of Donna,
I went to our café one day, they said that Donna walked away,
You think at least she might have stayed to drink her afternoon tea.

I'll take afternoon tea, if you'll take it with me,
You can take as long as you like because I like you, girl.
I take afternoon tea every day of the week,
Please come along if you like because I like you, girl.

The Million-Pound Semi-Detached

Angela and Derek had moved to the spacious, leafy suburbs of North London when Derek was demobbed after the Second World War. It had been a struggle when they first moved there. Derek worked long hours overtime in a local auto-repair shop so he could pay the mortgage. Angela took all the cleaning jobs she could get and worked at a nearby transport caff for a little extra. Derek was determined to make a go of it and studied at the local evening institute to become a qualified car mechanic. It was tough, but somehow they muddled through.

The struggle was not just financial. The neighbours were different. It was difficult to fit in at first. The whole lifestyle was more leisurely. Angela suspected that the people next door looked down their noses at them. Nothing was said to their faces, but there were those long, condescending looks and polite but silent nods every time they met a neighbour in the street. The house was worth it, though.

The first thing that struck Angela was the sense of calm that went through her as soon as she walked in. There was an almost religious feel to the house. It was not large by any means, but compared to the cramped terraced house in King's Cross, the semi in N2, East Finchley, was palatial. Angela particularly liked the front room in East Finchley. It had a large window that looked on to a small gravel path and was sheltered from the noise of the traffic from the main road by an avenue of large oak trees. It was like living in the city and the country at the same time. That was the attraction of the suburbs, neither here nor there, in the middle of someplace.

Angela would sit in the front room and look out of the window, on to the street and the passers-by. Derek would be in the back garden pruning his rose bushes, mowing the lawn. Angela's mum would often come up from Caledonian Road to visit, and the two of them would sit there for hours, fantasizing about who might have lived in the house before. They imagined themselves transported to another time. When polite gentlemen walked genteel ladies down a Regency street; horse-drawn carriages; men in top hats escorting ladies who wore dresses of crinoline, chiffon and lace. East Finchley seemed so far away from the London Angela knew – bomb sites, and back-to-back tenements with outside toilets. Leftovers from the Industrial Revolution. The war had driven Angela and Derek to the suburbs. Her mother marvelled at how, compared to central London, it had been relatively unscathed by the Blitz.

Two children were born in quick succession. By the time the mortgage had been paid off, the children had grown up, married and had families of their own. Derek had retired and they both felt it was time they moved to a more manageable property, a bungalow in Littlehampton perhaps, a cottage in Hastings. Mum had moved to a small flat up the road. She would be disappointed, but Derek and Angela knew it was time to sell the semi and move on. The house felt empty without the kids and even though they visited, the semi felt too big most of the time. Angela was alone with Derek now, and getting to know each other again would be easier elsewhere, less nostalgia.

The local estate agents looked over the property, in the cupboards and under the stairs, in the attic rooms the children had grown up in. They were just rooms to the estate agent. The surveyor prodded the walls looking for dry rot and woodworm. His assistant recorded the dimensions. A strange, impersonal ceremony. The estate agent congratulated Derek on the number of original features. The Regency bay window with its wooden shutters still functional, the original fireplaces and brass door-knobs.

Angela had felt a little embarrassed when she showed the estate agent the children's old bedroom. She had noticed it before, but after all those years, there still seemed to be the faint smell of nappies. She quickly went over and opened a window in case he commented, but it was all part of his job. She didn't like strangers looking around the house. Her memories were too alive.

The following week a large brown envelope arrived from the estate agent containing a brochure on the house. There was a photograph on the front which made the house look very elegant, fit to be in *Country Life* or the *Sunday Times* property section. Somehow the photograph didn't convey the homeliness and the comfort of the house. It made the property look a substantial investment rather than somewhere to live. Derek supposed the agents knew what they were doing. The wide-angle-lens shot from the rear of the house to the end of the garden made the freshly mown ninety foot of grass look like a lush cricket pitch. The only things missing were the croquet hoops.

Angela read the details. Little cupboards became storage areas. The attic room became a granny flat. Things that Angela and Derek had taken for granted over the years were itemized and given official names. Washroom, laundry, playroom. It made the house feel different. Their small living room off the kitchen was, according to the leaflet, in need of redecoration, and 'lived in'. Derek's junk room was a useful storage space. The children's old bedroom was a second bedroom. But then, at the bottom of the page, was written, 'an excellent opportunity to redevelop and to turn into flats'. When Angela showed Derek, he looked at it silently. His hands started to shake. He sounded angry when he spoke.

'Maybe it's for the best, I don't know.'

The estate agent had advised them to put the house up for auction.

'The market will take it. Property is on an up at the moment. Increasing in value by almost £1,000 a week. We could go through the roof with this one.'

Derek had grown up in another time. A fair price was a good price. But this was 1987, the property boom was in full swing. The Big Bang had hit the city. People were becoming millionaires overnight. Some fast-living city slicker probably earned as much in a week as Derek did in a year. Derek tried not to feel bitter about this.

'These are the times,' he pondered. 'I suppose we must move with them.'

He was sitting looking out the back window. Angela was making tea in the kitchen and could barely hear him.

'Haven't we come a long way since we started out? Now we're letting it all go.'

Angela brought over a cup of tea and placed it in front of him.

'The journey's not over yet, love,' she said comfortingly. She knew it would be a challenging time for their marriage. They had, in a sense, gone as far as they could go, even though Derek talked about travelling the world, going on a cruise, starting a small business. They both knew Derek wasn't strong or young enough to start up in business. Shortly before his retirement, he had been suffering from high blood pressure and had a few fainting spells. He tried to be philosophical.

'Maybe we were here just to look after this house till somebody else came along.'

He went into the back garden to prune the roses and tried to forget the property value of the house.

A few days later, the telephone started ringing. The estate agent was lining up lots of viewings. The first knock at the door was from a young, very well-to-do couple. He was obviously something in the City. She had a foreign accent, possibly Polish or Czechoslo-vakian. She spoke in broken English. She looked at the stains on the wall in the children's bedroom rather disapprovingly. He sniffed every time he walked into a room. They hardly said a word – it was as if Angela was a servant showing them around. They left rather quickly. Didn't even look back. Angela hoped they wouldn't buy it.

The next person was a woman almost Angela's age. Alone. Seeing the house for somebody else, probably her employer. When she showed an extraordinary interest in the attic room, Angela thought that she might be a granny coming to look at the house for her grandchildren. When she commented on the neat-and-tidy condition of the kitchen, Angela assumed that she was a housemaid or cook, and that's where she would be working. When she was leaving she explained she had recently been widowed and was looking for somewhere to start a small bed and breakfast. All those assumptions, but people are unpredictable. Weeks went by and there was an endless stream of viewers. After a while all the faces looked the same. Nobody stood out. Angela and Derek had the tour worked out, acting as guides.

They had a wager on who would buy the house. Perhaps it would be the foreigners, or the young couple obviously trying to buy their first house. That would have been nice. Another young couple starting again. Young hopefuls looking forward to a happy marriage and life together. At the end of the day it would be down to money, who would be prepared to pay the price. They knew that. The young couple had made an acceptable offer, but there was a last-minute hitch with the young man's medical, and his mortgage fell through. The estate agent thought that this would benefit everybody, because now the house could definitely be put up for auction.

The telephone rang and an excited young gentleman from the estate agency came on the line.

'There is an offer in the pipeline, and if we hold out until just before the auction we might be able to push them over the reserve price.'

Derek was unsure whether this was good or bad news. The estate agent explained that property was shooting up so fast that simply stringing out the sale for a couple of days could put £10,000 on the price. Derek mulled it over. He'd wanted to put the house on the market and sell it to the highest bidder. The thought of playing poker with the house had not occurred to him. He called the estate agent back to tell him he would rather wait for the auction date. If this person was still interested, they could buy the house there and then. The thought of a price war at this late stage was a little too stressful for him and his wife. The estate agent agreed and said he would contact the interested party.

The day before the auction, Angela was out of the house, and Derek was alone upstairs, looking through some old photographs, clearing out the attic. There was a knock at the door. He slowly walked down, half expecting whoever it was to have gone, but when he opened the door he saw a young girl, about seventeen or eighteen. She was unkempt, and at first he thought she was a beggar or a gipsy. She said she wanted to see the house, and this made Derek smile.

'Do you have an appointment?' he asked.

'No,' she said. 'But I would like to see the house very much.'

The girl looked like she was from another country, a refugee, but her accent was pure London. He should have phoned the estate agent to get clearance, but she looked harmless enough, so he let her in. She walked into the house as if she knew the place. Instead of looking around the house as if for the first time, it was as though each room held a memory for her.

Derek rarely offered people drinks, but he felt sorry for the little waif and offered her some tea. He wanted to know more about her. When he came out of the kitchen, he found her looking at the family photographs on the wall, touching them gently as she went from one to another.

'Such a beautiful family. There is so much happiness in this house. It's a pity you have to sell it.'

They sat down. Derek watched the girl as she sipped her tea.

The atmosphere seemed unreal. There was a strange glow around her, silhouetted by the afternoon sun. The girl knew he was staring at her but didn't seem to mind. She reminded him of someone he had known long ago, when he was a child.

'Do I know your parents? Are they coming to live with you?'

The girl looked confused. 'My parents? I have no parents.'

'Can you afford to buy this house?'

The girl smiled and put down her tea.

'I have means. I would like to make it clear now, sir. I would like to offer you a million pounds for your house.'

Derek almost dropped his cup.

'A million pounds? The reserve price is only £350,000!'

She smiled again.

'A million pounds. It's worth it to me.'

Derek explained that he couldn't alter the price or the terms of sale, but she should attend the auction in two days. She could save herself some money.

The girl was adamant.

'A million pounds, but I want everything left as it is. I want you to leave all your belongings, all your personal items, right down to the photographs, your clothes in the wardrobe. Everything.'

'You haven't seen the whole house. Please look around before we discuss an offer.'

The girl got up and walked towards the window.

'I know what is in the house.'

She went on to describe every room, every little detail. She even knew why and when Derek and Angela had moved there.

'You came here to get away from the bombs and the poverty in London, didn't you? You thought this would be a great place to raise a family, and it was. You wanted two kids, a cat and a dog. The same dream as everybody else, and you got it, didn't you, Derek?'

It was the way she said 'Derek', as if she knew him. When she left, she turned and smiled as she walked up the gravel path. Derek waved goodbye and closed the door gently. As he walked back into the front room, his head started to ache and his thoughts became muddled. When Angela got back she found him asleep in a deckchair on the lawn. He said nothing about the dizzy spell or the young girl.

That night, Derek had a dream about her. He was walking down a long country lane, and he saw the girl in the distance, in a long, blue dress. It was almost as if she was slowly dancing as he walked towards her down the path. In the dream he asked her who she was. She simply smiled and assured Derek that she had always been close to the house. She pointed over her shoulder. They were outside his own house. The large old semi she had offered a million for.

'It's not worth a million pounds, my dear,' Derek whispered to the girl.

'To me it will always be worth a million.'

The girl took Derek by the hand and walked him down the gravel path to the front door.

'I understand,' said Derek. 'You lived here in the past.'

'I haven't moved in yet, but you will know when you see me again.'

The following morning, Derek sat at the breakfast table and tried to explain the dream to Angela

'I'm sure she is the one who should buy the house. I wouldn't dream about her otherwise. The bricks and mortar can't be worth a million, but you can't put a price on memories. But if that's what she wants to pay, I suppose she can have it.'

He wondered whether he should tell the estate agent about the girl's offer or whether she would do a deal. Nobody could begrudge them making a little extra profit on the sale. What's a million pounds compared to a life's work? She could pay the asking price, and then secretly pay Derek and Angela the rest. It was probably just instinct, but he called the estate agent and told them he was taking the house off the market.

Weeks went by, but the girl never came back. Derek started thinking he'd been imagining things. Surely the house wasn't haunted. The people who had sold the house to them were a retired couple. No clues to the girl in blue there. Derek needed the sale to buy a bungalow they'd found in Sussex. The owners were pressing to exchange. Derek had always been cautious, and something told him to hang on. There was so much wrapped up in the property. A mistake now would affect their standard of living for the rest of their lives. They waited, but there was still no sign of the girl. The house went up for sale again. The property market was reaching its peak, and it couldn't stay this high for ever.

'We'll sell the place to the first person who offers a fair price.' Derek hung up the phone resolutely – there would be no further delay.

The telephone rang again almost immediately. Derek and Angela looked at one another, somehow knowing that it was bad news. Angela's mother had been taken ill a few weeks before and now she was in hospital for tests. The results were in: the tests were positive; the disease was terminal. The doctor explained that it would be over very quickly, so there was no need to keep her mother in hospital. She should be with her family for her last few weeks. Angela said she'd come and collect her, and bring her mother's belongings from the flat up the road. Derek was irritated by the news.

'This will put the kibosh on the sale. We'll never get rid of the place now, not with an old woman dying in the house. Why did I let this happen?'

Angela was too concerned about her mother to even answer back. She put up a bed in the front room so her mother could look out of the window at the trees and the passers-by. She would be out of the way if anyone came to view the house, and it was quick for the doctors too.

The date set for the new auction was approaching. So many people had seen the house, and despite Angela's mother being in the front room, the estate agents remained confident. Derek was anxious. He dreamed of the girl each night, but she had never come back. She hadn't contacted the estate agents. No more million-pound offers. It had been a ridiculous dream. Perhaps his mother-in-law brought him bad luck. She was recovering slightly. She'd been in the front room for only a week and the doctor couldn't believe how well she looked. He was very cautious about saying 'recovery', but he looked more optimistic each day he came.

'Your mother is a tremendous fighter. She's so happy here.'

Later that day the estate agent called with more bad news. The market was slowing down, and there was concern about the house reaching its reserve price. Derek went to the pub to drown his sorrows. He blamed Angela's mother, her illness, his own stupidity in believing in the girl in blue and the million-pound offer. He muttered angrily to himself on the way home, but as soon as he opened the front door he knew something more was wrong. Angela's mother had taken a turn for the worse. Angela was on the phone to her family in tears. Derek's dream that night was even more surreal. The girl was still in blue, and she was sitting at Mother's side. The girl was in a blaze of light, and the old woman was smiling at her, almost laughing in anticipation of something. The girl spoke softly.

'Are you afraid?'

Mother smiled, closed her eyes and went to sleep.

Derek woke with a jolt. The sheets were soaking with sweat. He reached out for Angela, but she was already up. He threw on his dressing gown and rushed downstairs. Angela was at her mother's side. The doctor had already arrived and pronounced Mother dead, and was just leaving as Derek entered the front room. The doctor took him to one side, gave him the details and the time, a few comforting words, and let himself out.

Other relatives arrived, funeral arrangements were made and the grieving process begun. Angela called her brother Les in America to get him home in time for the funeral. Derek had called the estate agent and informed him to put the auction on hold.

Later that night, Derek sat in the kitchen with Angela. They were exhausted but neither was able to sleep. Angela said her mother had said something about getting ready to cross the street for the last time, and a beautiful girl in a blue gown helped her.

The day before the funeral, there was a knock at the door. Derek opened it and saw the couple whose mortgage had fallen through. The young man had been left some money and could now afford a down payment. Derek told them about his mother-in-law, and they were content to wait for the sale. It seemed right to sell the property to a young couple as they had once been.

'They remind me of us,' said Derek. 'They have it all ahead of them.'

It would be difficult for them at first.

◼

Haven't we come a long way
From newly-weds in our bed-sitter flat?
We skimped and scraped every penny
For a down payment on our semi-detached.
New towns for all the young hopefuls,
A garden suburb with mortgage attached,
Oh, look at us now, sale all agreed, now it's time to exchange the
    contracts
With the proud owners of our million-pound semi-detached.
He came straight out of national service,
Demob suit and short back and sides,
And saw the bomb sites turned air-raid shelters,
Where their families lived all of their lives.
Then the nation built them a utopia,
With pebbledash on the outside, oh,

Look at them now, they've come a long way, they are affluent
   and bursting with pride.
Soon we'll be sitting inside that million-pound semi-detached,
Looking back at the past of this million-pound semi.
Two up two down, a back garden, that was the dream,
Two kids, a cat and a dog, that was the scheme.
Then the kids both grew up and got married and moved out of
   home,
Then we were strangers again, together alone.
Look at us now, what are we like,
Sitting alone in our million-pound semi-detached?
But the people who sold us our million-pound semi
Are all taking early retirement, the sum total of all of their lives.
Now the country is fat with inflation, immigration has helped
   them survive.
Once an Englishman's home was his castle,
Now it's a freehold investment to buy, oh,
Look at us now, debts all paid off, and the Empire has really
   struck back.
We're the proud owners of a one-million-pound semi-detached,
So detached in that million-pound semi-detached.
A new generation is buying and starting anew,
And learning by all their mistakes the way people do.
Like all the young hopefuls we're buying the future from you,
One day we'll understand what you've both been through.
Look at us now, what are we like,
Together alone, in our million-pound semi-detached?

My Diary

It was time to close another deal. Time to focus on Les Mulligan. Richard Tennant took out his notebook and continued his diary.

16 April

Flew back to LA to finalize contract for Les Mulligan.

Checked into and straight out of hotel. Air conditioning stank of perfume. Moved to the Peninsula.

Can't sleep. Les called. Sounded different again. Talking about some ghost in his work. Something about an evil spirit he picked up on the Underground. Will have to kill something off before he can do something new. Get some things out of his system. He sounds very confused. It's almost as though his personality changes every time he starts a new project. He gets overpowered by the characters he writes about. Manage to calm him but end up having to drink half a bottle of brandy and take a sleeping pill myself.

17 April

These dreams go on. I see my father sending me off to boarding school. Mother is so unhappy. I love her very much and yet she is afraid to show me any affection in case Father gets angry with her.

Surely they didn't think that I failed them? Father never forgave me for not following him into the clergy. He always looked down on my wealth. Said I missed my calling. Maybe I have a different calling. Helping lost souls like Les Mulligan. Must sleep. Morton Sosa tomorrow. Must close the deal.

18 April

Lunch with Morton Sosa and his contract people. Annette couldn't make it. The deal looks good, though. They really want to hear some of Les's new songs. Sosa keeps saying 'cutting edge', implying hard rock. Keeps pounding his fists on the lunch table emphasizing those powerful drum beats he's expecting to hear on Les's records. I'll have to play for time – he's incapable of writing his name at the moment, let alone 'cutting-edge' songs.

Back at the hotel I phone Les to see how he's doing. Get the speech about being pursued by some of his characters. Try to get him to focus on new people and forget the hangovers from his past. Sometimes he makes me feel like he's using me as a subject.

19 April, 4.32 a.m.

Worst dream yet. I am not really alive. I am an idea trapped in Les Mulligan's head. He's cast me as a benevolent businessman circum-navigating the world like a mixture of Don Quixote and Phileas Fogg, helping artists pursue their battle against evil tyrants like Morton Sosa. Then, Les leaves me with his unresolved characters to wander around Waterloo station until he is ready to work on them again.

Call home. Speak to Jenny. Says it's nice to be in touch again. Boys both doing well at school. Fees have gone up. (What's new.) Wishes things between us could be as they were before the divorce.

(She's still seeing Clive, though. I expect I'm paying for him as well.) I'll probably have to sell the house in Sussex. Bastard. *I must close another deal! Les! Where are those fucking songs!!!!*

20 April

Met Arnold Goodman from the Goodman agency. Wants me to run the UK operation for him. Nice chap. Great offer. Wrong time. Phone Les. No answer. Phone Miami. Leave for Florida in the morning.

Front desk send up a Fedex. It's a tape from Les. Inside is a letter to read while I play the tape. Also some lyrics to a song that doesn't seem to be on the tape: 'I'm scattered here, I'm scattered there, Bits of me scattered everywhere . . .'

24 April

Miami. Get a call from the office to say that Les has been seen wandering around Waterloo station, busking. Then he put himself in a rest home for a week to get away from some demons he met in the Underground. (Perhaps I should ask for my commission on his takings. That should snap him out of his delusion.)

2 May

Phone call from Los Angeles. Les arrested in Comedy Store on Sunset Strip after shouting abuse at a stand-up comedian. He claimed he was having a drink in the Hyatt House bar with Keith Moon. 'Moony took me to the club and made me do it.' Oh dear. Keith Moon has been dead for years.

3 May

Call Sosa. Explain that the Comedy Store incident was a publicity stunt. I thought Sosa would want to back out of the deal, but he laughed, saying it was 'fantastic'. Would only serve to broaden Les's appeal.

4 May

Finally speak to Les. (He called collect from a payphone in San Francisco.) Claims not to remember the incident. He was only trying to shake off another character who was out to get him.

12 May

Les seems more coherent today. He's in New York working on a new demo of his song. Asked me not to bother him with contracts. United want the thing signed but Les is stalling. Need to close. Phone Miami. All systems go. Everybody just waiting for me to say go.

Just received a reassuring phone call from Annette Fabrizzi telling me not to hassle Les while he's working. Can't help feeling she's playing the nice guy. Meanwhile Sosa and his attorneys are piling on the pressure. They know I know what they really want, but I'll be damned if I'll do the catalogue deal before we have new product and Les signs long-term with me. He says get the new album out of the way first. That's if he ever starts recording it. Dr Neuberg's office called. Need me to go in for more tests. No time. Called office. A band called Reflected Eyeballs phoned. Wanted to be represented by the man who manages Lester Mulligan. Bloody Mulligan. The has-been.

25 May

Read through Les's recording contract. United's standard agreement. None of the special concessions I promised. I'll have to try to put something in, otherwise he won't sign. Call Sosa. He's impatient but understanding. Says provided the product is hard, cutting-edge stuff. I keep hearing Sosa saying 'cutting edge', and I haven't the courage to tell him Les is over the edge.

Just received a fax from Les. He's writing a series of hymns. (Oh God. Wait till Sosa finds out.) Why do I bother? What's he got on me? The music still gets me. Makes me think of what it's like, growing up in a society with different values, different standards that music rebelled against. Maybe it's the past talking, our age. We seem to need to communicate with each other.

1 June

Just closed the three-picture soundtrack deal with Warner's. Only hope the creative people can deliver.

Reflected Eyeball's first single is highest chart entry of the week. Not a bad day. They expected Les to go to their gig, but he never turned up.

18 June

A reissued soundtrack I helped package has just gone into the US charts. Really should get Les to re-record all his old hits. Sosa seems to have forgotten all about 'Waterloo Sunset'.

21 June

A Fedex arrived at breakfast. Les sent me a couple of songs and a shirt from H & K for my birthday. The boys called. On the mobile. I expect the bill to follow later. Along with Jenny's expenses for the month.

Miami called. The boat is ready to go. Pity I might not be there for the trip. Come to think of it, I might not even be here. I should feel satisfied. Two bands in the charts. But Les still hasn't delivered. Says he's missing the vital mixture. He'd better do something soon. This diary is nearly full. And each day, my world is draining.

4 July

Sosa called. Has received Les's rough comp of songs with no 'Waterloo Sunset'. Says no 'Waterloo Sunset', no album. Tried to get hold of Les but he's disappeared. He left his apartment for London without warning. The whole deal could be in jeopardy. It's not the money. It's becoming something more.

5 July

Passed out last night. Couldn't get out of bed this morning. Pains everywhere. Call Miami. They'll have to go ahead as planned, but without me.

13 July

Spoke to Les. He doesn't want United to have 'Waterloo Sunset'. Says it's his. Says it's best to let people remember the original. Too many dreams are locked up in it. Will not translate nowadays. Well. That's the deal blown. Leave it for a few days then threaten to sue. That should send him scurrying into the studio. Dreams or no dreams.

14 July

Les sent a song. Says it's based on me. Also a note saying that he had gone back to London to reconsider. He wants to meet me at Waterloo station before closing the United deal. He says it's time. Check diary. Fits in OK. Between buying Lisson Grove properties and my operation. Called Sosa. Not in. Called Fabrizzi. She's delighted. Had dinner with David Muller. Wants me to broker an indie label based in Liechtenstein. Phoned Jenny but Clive answered so I hung up. Phoned Miami. The boat left safely. Without me. Thought about Les's note. I decide not to let him back down for the sake of the deal. They'll have to give him better terms. Didn't have a single drink today. Took my medication.

Played Les's song just before I went to bed. I felt rather insulted by it. He thinks he knows me! How dare he? But how on earth did he know about my diary?

I looked in my diary, no spaces today,
A life so eventful, stacked with appointments too important to
    break,
Lunch at the bistro, tea at the Savoy café,
No time to contemplate the isolation,
No second can be wasted, no space to think because,
My diary is full but my life is empty.
It's all so trivial really, the sheer pretension of it,
It's all so temporary, but all so shallow really,
Let me look, I might be able to squeeze you in between,
No, my diary is so full I couldn't possibly meet you today,
This evening is blocked out with potential investors in my lonely
    one-man play,
Perhaps next week maybe when there are fewer functions to
    attend,
So for now I'll pencil you in,
Between the visit to my doctor, my appointment at the bank,
This time it's really crucial, that's why it's written in red,
My diary is my life and my life is standing on my head,
Oh my diary is full but my life is empty,
Oh yes my diary is full but my life is empty,
I look at your picture on my bedroom wall,
I try to forget you, that's why my diary is full,
Chock-a-block with engagements but it's only a show,
Because I'm all dressed up with nowhere to go,
To hide my isolation, keep myself occupied,
My diary is my one salvation,
Names, dates, numbers, but inside I long to cancel all those
    entries,
My diary is full but my life's empty,
My diary is full but my life is empty.

Driving

It was love at first sight. It always was. Lawrence was an incurable flirt. Eye contact with a pretty woman was not enough; the look seduced him and he had to have her. It was out of his control. It was the same with the Bentley. He saw it in a showroom window in Potters Bar. A second-hand S type, the first of its line, the original, classic Bentley design, black with brown-leather interior, built around 1960. He saw it, it seduced him, he had to have it. Beg, borrow or steal, whatever it took. It had to be his. There was no question he could afford it. Business was on the up in the rag trade, and a company car could be written off against tax.

He could remember watching his father as a child, polishing his second-hand Ford Anglia on Sunday afternoons. It was his pride and joy. All else was envy and bitterness. He'd scowl every time a neighbour drove past in a better car. Afterwards it was an outing to the coastal towns of Southend and Dover. The playground of most East Londoners after the Second World War. In an hour and a half you could be in the Kursal fairground riding on the dodgems and the Tunnel of Love. Cockles and mussels off a stall by the sea. Schoolboys with legs chapped by the wind and sun. An afternoon stroll by the sea at Southend, and ice cream and candyfloss for the kids before Dad hustled them back into the car for the final drive home to Chigwell. The kids would be half asleep in the back, their young mouths smelling of sweets, their lips stained by milkshakes. Odours of stale breath mingling with confectionery and innocent young farts wafting up from the back seat. Once home, Lawrence would climb the stairs with his two sisters. Hear his dad complaining to Mum about his lot in life.

'How can that Alf Wilson afford a car like that? He's no better than I am.'

Lawrence could only remember his father complaining. Complaints about Winston Churchill. How it was his fault that everyone was hard-up after the Second World War. Complaints about Clement Attlee and the Labour government, who had promised a new deal for the workers, a welfare state, free health care. Then to see the country overrun by foreigners. Pakistanis, Chinese, West Indians, Poles, Czechs and the rest. Lawrence's dad had a grudge to settle with the world. He felt cheated by society and let everybody know it. Lawrence vowed to himself never to go without. He began to despise his father's generation for tolerating the austerity of post-war Britain in the vain hope that the Empire would return, and with it, a new prosperity for all. His father was a staunch member of the Printers Union and, out of frustration, even joined the Communist Party but, like all the other dissatisfied members of his generation, did nothing to change the world for himself. All Lawrence's father had was envy and bitterness, but his Ford Anglia was his pride and joy.

The only time Lawrence had seen his father genuinely happy was when he read through the motoring magazines looking at all the latest designs from overseas, and then he was happy to be venting his spleen. The cadillacs were a product of mercenary America. It had made all the money out of the Second World War, and left Great Britain to languish in debt. He was even more verbal about his European allies.

'Don't ever buy any of that continental rubbish – Volkswagen? Bloody Hitler designed the Volkswagen. That Fiat crap – you might as well put it straight on the junk heap. It can't compare with a good British motor. When you grow up, Lawrence, I want you to be proud to be British. Fly the flag. Buy yourself a patriot's car. You be a high flyer – get a Rolls or a Bentley.'

Lawrence had quite liked the American cars' flashy exteriors, but in a strange way he felt loyal to his dad. At the same time he was confused as to why his father just complained and did nothing. He'd never have a Bentley. He should have just taken what he wanted. His mother, on the other hand, had always encouraged Lawrence to take whatever he could from life. She had always given him what he wanted, and sown in him her golden rule: Envy is wicked; take what you want from the world and envy no one. You're as good as the next if not better. So why let a temptation pass by? She hadn't wanted him to turn out like his father.

The first time Lawrence saw a Bentley was in *Picturegoer* magazine. Dad had bought it after a matinée at the Granada cinema in the high street. A film star was sitting in the car with a glamorous woman. Lawrence was spellbound; it was all he wanted. To be a handsome matinée idol, the proud owner of a luxurious Bentley with a beautiful girl at his side. That was Everyman's dream after the Second World War.

To Lawrence's father's generation, women were second-class citizens; they'd accept what you were and what you had as long as you married them. Now, you had to have something to offer, some wealth. Lawrence had learned how to chat up girls, to take what he wanted from the world. To Lawrence's father's generation, the class system was there to balance society. Now, you could jump rank. When he left school at fifteen, Lawrence had taken an apprenticeship at the printing works. He'd left after six months. It wasn't enough. He'd started working in the rag trade in London's East End. The world had changed since his father's day. A hard-working man could reap his reward. Luxuries that were out of his dad'sreach were well within Lawrence's grasp. A television? Lawrence had two of them. His wife had a washing machine and a dishwasher. They enjoyed every luxury of the suburban family. It wasn't enough.

Lawrence's dad had died many years earlier. He had suffered a coronary at work, fallen over face down as he was setting up the printing blocks. They carried him to the undertaker with words printed all over his face. Lawrence had seen his father before he had been cleaned up and had even managed a little chuckle at the cruel, sad irony of it all. That was when Lawrence first heard the voice inside. A deep, authoritative voice that somehow seemed able to tap into Lawrence's psyche. To make up his mind whenever he was in doubt. An unseen friend and adviser. He had never forgotten his mother's advice: Act on impulse, take what you want; but his loyalty to his father had held him back. With his father gone, the voice could come to the surface, no doubt would confront it. His father was everything safe and ordinary. There was no way that Lawrence was going to end up like him. Now he could show his mother that he had learned from her upbringing. Lawrence had become a man of instinct. Randomness became his way of life, chance his master.

'Why not buy a Bentley, make your mother smile?' the voice said.

He was happy to comply. That weekend Lawrence's wife Joan was nudging the Bentley into the narrow driveway. The neighbours looked on a little enviously as the car came to rest outside the small detached house. Lawrence sat back in the comfortable leather passenger seat. He'd achieved what his father could only dream of. The next day they decided to take his mother for a spin. He sat in the back with her. She looked embarrassed to be in such a grand carriage, but the smell of real leather, the plush carpet, the sturdy wooden drinks cabinet, won her over. They made the car seem truly British, something to be proud of. It gave her a feeling of permanence. For Lawrence, it was *the* prize, the sign that he was a high flyer. Business was on the up. He employed twenty-five girls in the factory. The sky was the limit. The Bentley became the whole focus of Lawrence's life. It was becoming his obsession.

There was only one thing missing in his life now, and the Bentley would enable him to get it – a mistress.

It was love at first sight. It always was. Laura was a fashion rep from Essex, much younger than him, very ambitious and keen to get on in the world. She knew he was married, but couldn't ignore his interest in her. Laura was like the Bentley, a status symbol. Tall, young, athletic, and very, very sexy. She was slightly taller than Lawrence, now in his mid thirties. Laura had many admirers, men her own age, but Lawrence didn't worry about the wolf whistles, because there was no way these young studs could compete with him – he had the Bentley. He kidded himself she wanted him for his animal magnetism. He wanted her as an object, something that others would covet. Lawrence was perpetuating his father's envy, his need to have more than his neighbour. He was becoming everything he had once despised.

He was content enough to go back to his wife and children and play the part of the happy family man at the weekends, when he was cheating on his wife with Laura during the week. Joan was only the first reserve. His father had stifled his instinct back in those days. Lawrence had learned to act on impulse since then, to grasp the world by the scruff of the neck and not be held back by tiresome failings like fear. But there was one fear he couldn't conquer – driving. He was terrified of it, totally incapable. His instructor had advised him to give up after only two lessons. It upset Lawrence. His happy childhood memories were of watching his father drive the Anglia, of drives down to the coast, Mum sitting in the front handing out sandwiches and tea from a flask. But taking the steering wheel himself made him break out in a sweat. It was also beginning to affect his relationship with Laura.

During a dinner and dance at the golf club she confronted him. 'I see you and your wife driving around in that posh Bentley at weekends. Why don't you take me out in it? Are you ashamed of me or something?'

But there was no way he could admit that he couldn't drive. When Lawrence was out with his wife and children in the Bentley, everything was fine. With Joan at the steering wheel he felt safe, secure. It took him back to his own childhood. It was just the thought of driving himself. But an opportunity came out of the blue. His niece was pregnant and was marrying the father. A wedding had been hastily arranged in Hornchurch. Lawrence would be able to steal away from the hotel after a few drinks, take a cab back to Chigwell and meet Laura by the car, outside his house. He wouldn't have to drive it, he could make his conquest in the back seat. Things went according to plan. The cab dropped Lawrence at his house just before midnight, and Laura was waiting in the driveway. He made her walk with him across the flower beds, so the gravel path wouldn't crunch and disturb the neighbours. Laura stroked the car seductively. It was a truly sensual moment for her. Whatever affection she had for Lawrence was surpassed by her desire to make love in the back of the black Bentley.

Lawrence suddenly thought back to the picture of the film star in *Picturegoer*. At last he had fulfilled his dream. The car his father had always wanted, the woman he'd lusted after in his dreams. But this was no time to think about his father. As soon as Laura's body touched the fine leather upholstery, she seemed to melt into a mass of passion. She groaned as Lawrence reached down and slipped off her panties. He lifted them up, and in the half light, he could see that they were covered in a design similar to the Union Jack. 'Buy a Bentley. Fly the flag.' He'd cracked it.

It was pitch dark apart from the street lamp outside his house, but he could hear Laura breathing in and out, taking in the sweet smell of the leather. She pushed him over and smothered him in an aggressive embrace. He was overpowered by her perfume – strong, sweet and slightly cheap. The more he kissed, the more it rubbed into his own skin. On his skin, it seemed to metamorphose into a new odour, an odour from many years ago, a strong aftershave.

The sound of light breathing had detached itself from Laura. The two of them weren't alone. Lawrence opened an eye and saw the shadowy outline of a man sitting in the driver's seat. He quickly closed his eyes again. Laura was unphased, totally absorbed in frantic lovemaking. Then Lawrence heard the sound of a voice, a familiar voice, deep, dark.

'Take your hands off that girl, Lawrence, or I'll slap your arse.'

Lawrence's heart skipped a beat. Even Laura seemed to have stopped breathing. The car was silent.

'Who's that?' Lawrence whispered. Laura didn't hear. She was sucking Lawrence's neck.

'You know very well who I am, you young scallywag. I'll teach you to misbehave. I'll show you the back of my hand, you randy little sod.'

Lawrence jumped up in his seat. He leaned over to the driver's seat. There was nobody there. He pushed Laura aside and rushed out of the car. She followed him, protesting, rearranging her clothes.

'What are you playing at? Don't you fancy me?'

He was shaking uncontrollably. He was terrified. 'Did you hear that voice?'

'What voice? I didn't hear no bloody voice. What are you talking about?'

Lawrence felt faint. They walked around the block, Lawrence hoping the fresh air would clear his head. By now he felt slightly embarrassed about mentioning the voice. It was clear that Laura had been unaware of that other presence, and was unimpressed by his excuses of feeling faint. He took her for an Indian meal in the high street, and she went home happier, but unfulfilled. Lawrence was too terrified to go back to the house alone, but felt compelled to do so. As he walked towards the house, along the gravel path, he tried to avoid looking over to the Bentley.

The following Sunday, Lawrence's wife drove them to pick up his mum, and they set off for Brighton. The day went off without a hitch. Lawrence had bought some L-plates and took the wheel for a practice drive. Finally, he was in the driving seat. The road ahead seemed to open up. Then, as he made a turn, a loud voice bellowed around the car.

'Hit the little bastard in front. You're better than him. Kick the bugger off the road.'

Lawrence skidded the Bentley to a halt. Joan looked up.

'What's the matter, Larry? You nearly caused a crash.'

'Did you hear that voice?'

'I didn't hear anything.'

Joan took over the steering wheel, and carried on driving. Lawrence changed places with his mother. He was destined to remain in the passenger seat. It was, without a doubt, a family car. It was as if his father had somehow gained possession of the Bentley he had always wanted. But it was imbued with his father's jealousy. That, and Lawrence's loyalty to his father, would never allow him to drive the car. It was just like the old days. His father was back, doubt confronted him and stifled the voice of instinct.

■

Drop all your work,
Leave it behind,
Forget all your problems,
And get in my car,
And take a drive with me.

The sandwiches are packed,
The tea is in the flask,
We've plenty of beer,
And gooseberry tarts,
So take a drive with me.

We'll take your mother if you want to,

DRIVING

We'll have a picnic on the grass.
Forget your nephews and your cousins
And your brothers and your sisters,
They'll never miss us,
'Cos we'll be drivin'.

Thousands of trees,
Hundreds of fields,
Millions of birds,
So why don't you come
And take a drive with me?

We'll talk to the cows
And laugh at the sheep,
We'll lie in the field
And we'll have a sleep,
So take a drive with me.

And all the troubled world around us
Seems an eternity away.
And all the debt collectors, rent collectors,
All will be behind us,
But they'll never find us,
'Cos we'll be drivin'.

Past Barnet Church,
Up to Potters Bar,
We won't be home late,
It's not very far,
So take a drive with me,
Take a drive with me.
Drivin'.

Waterloo Sunset

The day was blurred. Like one of those old French Impressionist paintings where you're never sure whether the artist was drunk or needed spectacles. Fox strolled across his attic room to read the letter by the one dormer window. He peeled open the buff envelope and saw the hospital's headed paper. He set a kettle to boil. Normally he would hover impatiently, but today, he had more time. He listened intently as the water started to boil, then studied the steam as it curled out of the spout, until the force of the boiling water made the kettle splutter and shake. He'd never stopped to consider the physical process before. Full-fat milk. No need to worry about cholesterol now. He hadn't bothered to read the diagnosis when it had first arrived. He'd left it on the table at the side of his bed, and it had sat there like an unwanted intruder. He didn't know why he should read it today. He knew the contents: Results positive. Only the punctuation registered. The commas, a chance to take a breath or pause; the full stops, the end of a phase. Fox's body was coming to a full stop. He was in his final phase. Danger and the risk of death had been part of his life. The GBH and then the robberies. What he found difficult now was the clinical assessment, the parcelling out of time. It was as if there was an assassin waiting in the dark. He drank the tea as if it was his last. Looked at the world through his window and, back inside, through the frames of his paintings. He had imagined those worlds. They were places he had never been, the chronicle of his imagination in prison.

Fox considered himself a Londoner. Apart from a spot of porridge in Dartmoor and that awful time in Rampton, he'd lived in London all his life. But there were so many places he had never been – the Tower of London, the Houses of Parliament, Westminster Abbey. Overfamiliarity led him to take them for granted, even after years in prison. The marks persisted. His once elegant hands, an artist's hands maybe, fingers bloated by too many fights. He'd never let himself go to seed, even now he was on the way out. Cleanliness had helped him keep his dignity. It hadn't moved him any closer to godliness, though. He'd resisted the chaplain's persuasion, but now he wished he hadn't given religion such a wide berth. What would be left of him when he was gone?

He remembered the old song about two characters, Terry and Julie, who met at Waterloo Underground. The song had come on the radio while he was waiting in the get-away car at the Cannon Street robbery. He had been engrossed in it and hadn't noticed the police cars draw up. One of the policemen whistled the song as he took him into custody. A painting of that song should have begun his chronicle, but it had always eluded him. Maybe he should try once more.

He headed for the Embankment. It was undergoing a face-lift. The Houses of Parliament had been cleaned up, and the new site for Charing Cross station was nearly complete. The skyline was being altered by high-rise office blocks, but the Savoy still retained its dingy elegance. Fox wanted to convey a feeling of romance, but somehow he found himself concentrating on the isolated people walking along by the river instead of the warm feeling the song's imagery gave him. The people seemed lost, the same way Fox felt. He thought of the bag-woman he'd painted in Regent's Park. When he got back to his flat and tried to work on the picture, he got depressed. There seemed to be nothing but these sad people, the scene itself had no life of its own, no poetry. Maybe it was best left as an idea, maybe it couldn't be captured in an image. Suddenly, Fox felt pain shoot through his body. In his obsession with the painting he'd forgotten his illness. He had medication, but his body must have been becoming immune to it. He doubled the dosage and washed it down with half a bottle of vodka. The cocktail dulled the pain, but the bitterness seized him inside. Sod art. He was only a third-rate amateur. He wouldn't be remembered for his painting. He was a con artist. One last job. He'd have to spruce himself up.

He wandered down Marylebone High Street and saw a tuxedo in the window of a charity shop. It would be perfect. Next to it, on a mannequin, was an old ballroom gown, just like his mother used to wear. Sequins sewn on by hand, sections of lace, old embroidery. Slightly see-through – that must have raised the blood pressure of many a dance partner. He remembered that night. Fox and his mates had been jiving to rock and roll records, but had stopped dead in their tracks when his mum and dad had started waltzing. They seemed so affectionate, so in love. The tuxedo fitted Fox perfectly. The trousers were a little shiny on the backside, but otherwise the tux was in mint condition. There was a man's name inside, next to the maker's label. Geoffrey Sillet. Only a name. It said nothing about the person's life. Still, it was a good deal, and it made him feel debonair. Now, he'd be able to con his way back in with the high rollers.

It way have been the effects of the medication, but Fox could have sworn the doorman of the Savoy bowed as he walked in. It was like he was floating. The lobby was packed, but somehow the crowd parted as Fox waded through. Surely there would be some unsuspecting toff in the bar who Fox could take advantage of. Some eager do-gooder primed for a soft touch. He sat down next to a cultivated-looking type who was dressed for dinner. He was chain-smoking. Fox sized him up. He ordered a lager, and the man started talking to him. His name was Richard. There was a world of difference in their accents, but as Richard spoke Fox's initial dislike disappeared. He felt some empathy for the man. He was in the middle of a rather difficult negotiation and was waiting to meet a business partner in the bar. He seemed to identify with Fox too. They shared their cynicism for a world that seemed full of double standards. Fox talked about his life, how he had been repatriated through art. Richard talked about class. Even though he had been to a smart public school, he never finished 'the course'. He felt under-educated, out of step with people from the same background. He hadn't gone to university, hadn't gone for a safe establishment job. He envied people who made a living out of being creative. They filled all the gaps in his life, and helped uproot a society that appalled Richard. He'd been ostracized, but was happy to be an outsider. Money was a way of getting back. Fox couldn't have agreed more. This guy would be easy. Richard continued.

'I met this chap a while ago. Tracked him down in New York. He was a total wreck. Haunted, a little deranged. We came from totally different backgrounds and had nothing to connect us, but we both wore the same shirts, and that was enough. Somehow that gave us an insight into one another. We were meant to go on a journey together.'

Fox watched Richard as he searched his jacket pockets for a cigarette. He caught a glimpse of his wallet.

'The only problem was, neither of us was sure who was taking who. We envied each other's lives. He wanted my ability to do a deal, I wanted his creativity. Our meeting was premature, but we learned a great deal from each other. He confided many of his secrets to me. It turned out he was not quite the person I thought he was. Something in him had gone astray. Some sort of personal trauma that was too painful to confront. He'd gone inside his work so deeply, he'd surrendered his own character to his songs, and they lived through him instead of the other way around. He had become the characters he had invented. The lyrics in his songs spoke for him. He lost his own voice.

'I inherited only the shell. I tried to connect it with his everyday persona, and sometimes it seemed to work, but I always knew that the real creative part of him was down in the Underground, busking anonymously, away from the spotlight. That way he could sing songs about people without getting involved in their lives and getting hurt. Now, we have simply brought each other to this place, but still neither of us knows who is taking who.'

The bar was getting crowded. Richard's mysterious business partner still hadn't arrived, and he suggested that he and Fox take some air. They walked up the Strand, past Charing Cross, and looked at the river. The rush-hour traffic was in full flow, and the commuters were making their way across the bridge. Fox found himself being seduced by the view of London he'd been trying to capture. Richard was still smoking. He was talking about the river, saying he believed that it would always lead him to good fortune. They walked on, and reached a dark stairwell under Charing Cross Bridge. Fox felt it was time to take advantage.

'Could do with some good fortune myself.'

A stab of pain stopped him from overpowering his victim, and now Fox was helpless. Richard helped him up the steps, to the top of the bridge. Fox could hardly get the words out.

'I'm going to die.'

Richard smiled compassionately. His words shot through Fox more powerfully than the pain.

'You've actually been dead a while. You've just been waiting to be taken captive. In a moment. Like one of the pictures you paint.'

'Then why am I here? What am I waiting for?'

'You are waiting for that final moment. But you won't know for sure until you see that river stop. That's when you'll know he's finished. Your song is done and you can go home. Try not to build your hopes up. You're probably just another unresolved idea that will get shelved for another time. You'll be hanging around on this bridge for ever I expect. Just like me.'

Fox was grappling with what Richard was saying.

'You mean there's no escape?' Richard sighed.

'I thought there was once. I thought I'd made my fortune and would be sailing around the world on my yacht.'

Fox's face lit up.

'You have a yacht?'

'Yes. She's been having some repairs done. She's already left Miami without me. I thought she'd be my get-away. Unfortunately, it looks as though the next time I'll see her is when we sail up the River Thames.'

Fox came to a conclusion which alarmed him.

'Did you mention this yacht to this friend of yours?'

'Only in passing. Why?'

'No reason really. It just makes sense now how I decided one day to paint a picture. I'd never seen racing yachts but the image just came into my head. Sold the picture to a young couple for a tenner.'

Richard raised an eyebrow.

'Yes. Probably part of his plan.'

'Is that why I am here? So you can show me the way?'

Richard looked at Fox's tuxedo.

'Hardly think so. Although you do seem dressed for the occasion. Someone will recognize you by the tuxedo. They'll be dressed in one too. Probably by the same tailor.'

Fox felt dizzy and confused. Maybe it was the medication. Richard carried on talking.

'The lost people travel around on the same journey for ever. Trapped in their own hell on the Underground. It's not until they come up to the overground that they see the chance to be free. You see the people standing on the bridge looking at the river? They see their whole life flowing down that river and they come, and they look at it, and they see everything they ever wanted. You'll look at the river. Just stand and watch it flow. Slower and slower until it stops moving. You'll know when the time has arrived.

When the river stops. Just blink your eyes once and the image will stay with you.'

The setting sun lit Richard's face with an eerie glow. Fox felt the strength drain from his body.

'I'm not ready. God has no angel to guide me. I'll try and get to the hospital.'

Richard stared at Fox long and hard, and every emotion passed across his face. Then he looked away dispassionately.

'I have to make my appointment.'

Fox was still alert enough to be inquisitive.

'Who are you waiting for?'

'The man who wrote "Waterloo Sunset". I've been trying to coax him across the river. I've been in the bar at the Savoy every night, just as he said, but he never comes. He's not ready to leave the Underground.'

'Maybe I'll see him there,' said Fox. 'If I can't paint the picture, I'd like to meet the man who wrote the song.'

'I can't go down to the Underground with you. I spent too much time there.'

'You'll capture the picture in your own imagination, and there will be a space in it for you.'

Fox shook Richard's hand and left him on the bridge, cigarette in hand, looking at the river. Richard seemed at peace. Resigned.

Fox slowly walked across to Waterloo station. He just about managed to climb the steps under the clock and took the escalator down to the Underground. He heard the sound of gentle guitar-playing and was convinced he heard a choir singing. The medication was kidding him. There'd be no angels in hell. As he descended, the choir faded away and the dull roar of the Underground swelled. Fox thought he heard the screams of a torture chamber. Condemned commuters suffering hell's wrath. Or was it a train screeching to a halt? He saw a busker at the end of the corridor. He was singing something about commuters journeying through the underworld.

It sounded as if the lyrics were being sung in another language, but he could still catch the meaning. The busker tilted his head to look over his sunglasses and smiled at Fox. He said something without speaking, and Fox replied without a word. They walked out to Waterloo Bridge. Fox looked into the busker's sunglasses and saw the reflection of the sun setting over Waterloo. Even in the tinted glasses the light was too bright. The whole sky seemed to be on fire. Fox looked towards the brilliant light. He was caught in the moment and the river stopped.

Scattered
Home

All the children were home that day. It was strange to see the family gathering again. It seemed years since they had all been together. His sisters and brothers had got older and had families. The nephews and nieces had all grown up, and some of them had children of their own. Some had divorced. Time had stood still, apart from some wrinkled brows, grey hairs and a few paunches. Les knew the formula. It was almost as predictable as the suit he was wearing. The same for weddings, christenings and funerals. All the family assembled in the front room.

Outside the front door people were gathered in groups, catching up with gossip, remembering old times. The cars were parked up the side of the street, and some children were playing outside the house, unaware that it was a funeral.

Les had been abroad when his sister had called to tell him their mother was dead. He'd wanted to come back from New York earlier, but he couldn't get away. When his sister called, Les felt too numb to feel guilty about not being with his mum at the end. She would have been all right, surrounded by the rest of the family, but just the same, there was a niggling feeling inside him. Maybe he had let her down and disappointed her. He was her favourite, and he hadn't been there.

The welcome seemed almost rehearsed: 'Glad you could make it back, Les. Good that you're here.'

Les knew all the faces, but somehow didn't know the people. They were people from his childhood, faces he had grown up with.

They looked older, smaller somehow. In their presence he still felt like a child, and after they all got together in the back room and had a few drinks, the old stories would come out about Les as a little boy. He recognized the uncle who'd put sixpence under his pillow when his first tooth had fallen out. The cousin, Penelope, he used to have a crush on, and his brother-in-law, Scott, who had never got on with his mother. She'd never suffered fools gladly. His mother had always had the upper hand with Scott, could always out-shout, out-argue, outwit him. He seemed more relaxed now she was gone, but none the less he was grieving.

'Sorry to meet you in such tragic circumstances.'

Les touched Scott's arm and saw tears in his eyes.

The room was crowded now. But the focal point was missing. It was odd how just taking away one element, the whole chemistry of the company had changed. They always called her Mum, but today they referred to her as Mother. It was fitting for a strong character who dominated the company she was in.

His sister brought him a cup of tea. She spoke in a brisk whisper.

'She's still in the funeral parlour if you want to go and see her.'

Les was unsure. He knew he should go and pay his respects, but he didn't know how he would react. He remembered one aunt who'd broken down and tried to climb into the coffin with her husband. Les didn't want to make an exhibition. When Les's sister had said 'You want to go and see her?' it was as if she were throwing down the gauntlet, because he hadn't been there at the end. He felt as if the whole room had gone silent. He had to go, even though he was afraid. He didn't want to see the dead, he preferred to remember people as they were, living. His relatives watched as he left the house. Watching him do penance.

The undertaker was waiting for him outside a small parade of shops. He showed Les down the small dark corridor of what seemed like a converted terraced house. The undertaker paused at the door, then walked him to the room where his mother lay. Les noticed that the floor was covered in very cheap linoleum and he wished it had been carpet. He went up to the coffin and looked in. He felt a sharp pain in his head and heavy pressure in his chest. He fell on one knee, as if waiting for a knighthood, or forgiveness, or understanding. Then he plucked up the courage and looked at his mother's face. It resembled her, but it also resembled every relative he had ever known. There was something of her in all of them. He needed to look away. Then he started to feel dizzy, attempted to get up and almost fell over. The undertaker led him outside and asked if he was all right. Les smiled and thanked him, and left. The shock of seeing his mother seemed to clear a haze that had confused him for many months. On the way back to the house Les stopped off at his mother's flat. It was much the same as it had been when he was last there with her. Her photographs, her things, even her tea mug was where she had left it. He sat down in her armchair and, for a moment, nodded off. When he woke he half expected her to walk in with a cup of tea and a piece of fruitcake.

'Are you OK boy, is everything OK?'

Les couldn't believe how still the room was. The sun was gleaming through the curtains but there were no dust mites glistening in it. He looked in his mother's bureau and, under a pile of old letters, he found brochures on How to Live with Cancer and How to Cope in Times of Illness. His mother must have been ill for some time, but she hadn't told anybody. He also found a small gift his mother had wrapped for his daughter's birthday. She had always found room in her life to be a grandmother. And time to be stubborn. There was a cigarette stubbed out in the ashtray. She'd always kept some papers for him, in a small briefcase, in her closet. It was still there. When he was satisfied that everything was in order, he locked the door and made his way back to his sister's house.

The funeral gathering was complete. He cast his eyes around the family characters, looking for light relief, away from the grief welling up inside him. Aunty Ethel from Sidcup was devouring a sandwich.

She still hadn't got her teeth fixed. Two front uppers had broken off her dentures years ago. When she spoke she still whistled, like when he was a child, issuing forth lumps of wet ham sandwich. Cleaning up after Aunty Ethel was a family pastime. Poor cousin Muriel was already on her second packet of Kleenex. She had been put in a psychiatric hospital after a nervous breakdown. She was over fifty, but she still looked attractive to Les, ten years her junior.

'How's she doing, old Muriel? Still as nutty as a fruitcake?'

Angela led him into the kitchen for a quiet word.

'She says she's cured now, but between you and I, I think she's as barmy as she ever was. Poor thing can hardly put a sentence together. It's the drugs they give them.'

He went back into the room. He saw Victor. His cousin had recently got married, to a very attractive secretary. Victor had been to one of the most established public schools, and had a very effeminate manner. His hair flopped over one side of his face and made him look like a basset hound. Victor's father was the one member of the family who could even loosely be described as a professional. Some sort of dream doctor. He'd been a widower for many years, and he was lecturing abroad. He wasn't expected.

Les's sister Angela was starting to usher people out to the cars. Les took another look at everyone. All from his mother and father. Most of them at any rate.

Les was the last to leave. Angela locked up and got into the last car. Les walked slowly up the gravel path to join her, and heard those familiar echoing steps behind him as if somebody else was there. It was something to do with the large trees forming a tunnel, but today the sound took on a new significance. He asked about his cousin Lawrence. Angela said he would be coming along but had had a few last minute problems. Just as he was getting into Angela's car, he saw a large black Bentley. Lawrence had made it. His wife Joan was at the wheel. Scott was waiting in the car ahead, muttering depressing clichés. Les could hear what he was saying.

'Well, this is the last of the street. End of an era.'

Les looked at Angela.

'Not if I can help it. This will not be the last of the street.'

The funeral cortège slowly made its way up the street, past Mum's flat, past the pub where she often sat drinking a half-pint of Guinness, then on to the cemetery. An hour later, the cars were back at the house.

Les had suggested they play some records at the wake, some of Mum's old favourites, but Angela had said it would be disrespectful and make people over-emotional. It was the first family event without music that Les could remember. Perhaps some old songs would fill the gaps, identify an emotion, bring people together. No one dared mention the days when Mum would lead a singsong for the departed. She had been the life and soul.

Everybody looked old, but then there had always been a large age range in the family. He would run around with his nephew Sidney when they were children. They were always disrupting adult affairs, spilling drinks as they ran through the grown-ups' legs. He hadn't taken any notice of what adults did. He and Sidney had been the scourge of his mother, always causing chaos, everywhere they went, but now Mum was gone, and the few grandchildren were on their best behaviour. Les wished one of them would break out and cause a disturbance. Even Sidney had grown up, standing in the corner with his wife and children. Surely this wasn't the way to remember Mum. She wouldn't recognize everyone so well behaved.

But, somehow, time had also stood still. They were all gathered in a childish, innocent huddle, all joined in grief. The family had grown apart and gone their separate ways, but now they were united, able to talk together again. Old grudges were forgotten. There was even muted laughter. But through all the conversation, there still seemed regret about what hadn't been said. Those last words, final farewells. Les felt the guilt build up inside. He wished he had been there at the end. It was only a matter of time before somebody would have a go, or was it something else that would never be said?

Les returned to his mother's flat. The stillness bothered him, so he opened the window to give the place some air. He sat at the piano. It was a little upright they had played when they were children. It was almost disrespectful that there had been no music. Les sat at the piano and touched a couple of the keys. Then he played a few chords. There would be music at this funeral. At first he was going to play a solemn hymn he'd written, but then he remembered how his mother liked to dance. He remembered all the family parties and started thumping out an old rock and roll song. The piano was painfully out of tune, it had always been. The dissonance gave the sound a ghost-like quality. Then, a gust of wind blew a blast through the flat and the kitchen door slammed shut. It made Les smile. It was like a signal to finally release that unfinished song that had been going around his head for so long. He played the chords as hard as he could and laughed out loud. The kids were back causing havoc in the house.

To the fields we are scattered,
Then from the dust we are born,
We survive somewhat battered,
To a new life, a new dawn,
In the end what will it matter?
There'll only be my ashes to scatter,
And all the logical answers to a worrying mind,
Will be scattered in time.

Beaten and battered,
To the earth you are scattered,
You're going home so what does it matter,
To an atomic mind,
Scattered here while you travel time.